# Chapt(

**D**espite all his wanderings, his beloved Sussex Downs had always been the homing beacon in his head; he knew that it would reclaim him eventually. Nicholas Harrison was now retired after a life in many, varied jobs and in numerous different countries. He was sitting in the garden of his house in Poynings with its splendid view of the downs. As he gazed at the tree-flanked escarpment of Newtimber Hill, he reflected on his life which, he felt, had been an utter disaster.

He was born in 1950, second son of Mildred and Franklin Harrison. Beyond any doubt, the worst of many bad periods in his life was his miserable childhood. From an early age, his parents had made it very clear to him that he was a mistake; they had only ever intended to have one child – his brother Jeremy. While Nicholas might, perhaps, have expected some support from Jeremy, this never happened. He regarded Nicholas as an inferior being, and never let slip any opportunity to make him feel small and stupid.

Nicholas was sent away to boarding school when he was seven. When it had been announced to him that this was what was going to happen, although he felt scared and lost at the thought of it, he acknowledged to himself that it could not possibly be worse than staying at home. Indeed, when he started at Motcombe School in Warwickshire, he felt, looking back on it, that he had settled in remarkably quickly and soon found many 'brothers' who did not think he was a contemptible idiot, and actually seemed to like him. He enjoyed his classroom time and was eager to learn. No doubt this was, in part, due to a need to prove Jeremy wrong. In due course, aged 13, he passed his Common Entrance exam and moved on to Denport Abbey, a public school in Lincolnshire where he discovered his love for all sports and continued to make good academic progress, much to the freely expressed surprise of Jeremy and his parents. However, it was at Denport Abbey that his social life began to crumble. He made one or two friends, but was dismayed to find that most of his fellow-pupils were deeply irritating and often stupid. He sometimes reflected on whether this antipathy for his fellows, in some way, reflected his own shortcomings. But he always came to the conclusion that most of the other boys were indeed a hopeless lot. This opinion was almost always confirmed by the fact that the marks he received for his school work were higher than anyone else's.

In 1961, with the aid of a scholarship, he started at Loughborough College of Advanced Technology to pursue a three year course in engineering, finally achieving an honours degree.

The day he left home to start at Loughborough was the last time he saw or spoke to his parents or Jeremy. He was determined to take the opportunity to banish them utterly from his life. On the rare occasions that he subsequently reflected on this achievement he would casually wonder if they missed him at all and instantly knew that they did not. During the college vacations he managed to arrange that he could stay on at his term-time lodgings. To pay for the rent and to buy food and other essentials he was able to obtain temporary jobs with various businesses in Loughborough.

When he had finished at the college he was able to get an engineering job with a crane building firm in Leicester. What he regarded as his new-found wealth astonished and puzzled him. What on earth could one spend such money on? He had no idea, and began a life-long habit of putting a large part of his income each month into savings. He loved the engineering work he was doing, but the truly awful people he had to work with he found very trying. It was just the same as at school.

After only eighteen months at the crane factory he decided that he had to move on. He could not bear to work a moment longer with such trying and stupid people. It shouldn't be difficult, he thought, to find another job without too much trouble; after all he did have excellent qualifications and he knew that he was a good engineer.

And so it turned out. He moved further north to Manchester and got himself a rented bed-sit and a new job with another engineering company, with some hopes that he would enjoy the company of his work-mates. He was saddened to find that this was not to be the case.

So began a life-time of frequent job changes, enabled by the fact that he was, indeed, a good engineer and was almost always able to obtain excellent references from his previous employer. He lived in the slowly diminishing hope that somewhere there must be a group of intelligent and likable people. After his third job in Britain he decided that perhaps the problem was the British people. He emigrated to Australia and worked his way through several jobs there. He finally retired after living and working in Australia, Canada, the United States, Argentina, Germany and back again to Britain.

As Nicholas sat in his garden he was reminiscing about his life. It had been a pretty miserable life because of his problem with almost all of his fellow human beings. It gave him pain just to think about it. What on earth was wrong with him? He really needed to find out. Having plenty of time now to investigate, he started to explore the internet for relevant psychology articles and he spent many days in the Brighton reference library. Through his research he discovered that the root of his problem was the fact that his parents had taught him to hate and despise himself, and he knew that everyone he met would feel the same about him. To defend himself against this sea of hatred he pretended that he didn't care and ensured that he was beyond the reach of universal dislike by being better and brighter academically, and subsequently outperforming all his competitors in engineering. But he felt so very lonely. Apart from his research, his days were filled with long walks on the downs, and, when the weather wasn't so good, in his workshop at the back of the garden building immaculate miniature engines and vehicles of various kinds. And now, on this beautiful day on 13th August 2013, he was sitting in his garden soaking up the sun. That night when he went to bed he could hear the hoot of a tawny owl and, a little further away, the bark of a fox. He felt marinated in contentment. But he wasn't to know of the dramatic changes that were to befall him on the very next morning.

# Chapter 2

He knew that something was not right before he had opened his eyes. There was a strange smell; not unpleasant, just different. He opened his eyes. He wasn't in his own bed or his own house. He could not make out where he was until he realised that he knew that wallpaper. This was his childhood bedroom in Lewes. He leapt out of bed. He vaguely recognised the pyjamas he was wearing. He looked down at himself and found that he was only about five feet tall. His body was that of a child. "Oh God! Oh God! What the hell's going on?"

"Help! Help! Who's that? Where are you? What are you doing?"

Nicholas hadn't said that. His mouth was moving, but it wasn't him saying it. It sounded like a child. In fact, it was the same husky, childish voice that he had himself spoken with just now. Oh Lord, this can't be happening. It must be a dream. But, if so, it was a waking dream. He certainly had his eyes open and he was standing up. He pinched himself.

"Ouch! Who did that? Just go away or I'll call my father."

"No, please don't do that. I'm as much in the dark as you are, and I'm sure I'm every bit as scared as you are. Can we just sit down for a moment and talk to see if we can sort this nightmare out?"

"OK, I suppose so. But where are you? I can't see you. Please show yourself. I'm not going to talk to someone who is hiding."

"That's part of our problem," Nicholas replied. "I can't show myself. But please trust me. We must talk. I think I know who you are, but can you tell me your name?"

"It's Nick."

"I thought so. That's Nick Harrison, isn't it?"

"Yes. How do you know that?"

"To tell you that, I will have to tell you a bit about myself. I am an old man – sixty-three years old……"

"You certainly don't sound like it. You sound more like me…….Oh, Oh, Oh! You've been talking through my mouth haven't you?"

"Yes Nick, I'm afraid I have."

"Oh, that's horrible."

"I know. It must be. It's also horrible for me not to have a mouth or a body of my own."

"Oh shit! Do you mean that you are…..in my……in my head?"

"I don't know or understand anything of this. But yes, I think I must be in your head. I can't think of any other way I could speak with your voice. But let me tell you a little more about myself; it just may make it a little easier for you. Perhaps even for me. When I went to bed last night I was just an old man going to sleep in my cottage in Poynings. When I woke up this morning……Well you know about that. The most important point is…..Well I think it's important. My name is Nicholas Harrison."

"What do you mean? *My* name is Nick Harrison"

"Yes, that's right. I think we must both be the same person, but I am the person you will be when you are sixty-three."

"Oh that's ridiculous. That's totally impossible."

"I know Nick. I share your incredulity."

"Oh please! Don't start talking posh on me. I don't even know what that word means. How could I possibly have said that?"

"Because you didn't. I did, using your mouth and lungs and vocal chords. Because that is the only way I can speak now. Oh God this is so awful! The main reason I think that my being in your head is the only reasonable explanation is that when I woke up this morning I knew I wasn't in my own house or bed. Then I recognised that I was in my own childhood bedroom, and I saw that I was in a child's body. But there is one way I can prove it – to myself, anyway. Will you please go over to your mirror? I will recognise my childhood self if my theory is correct."

Nick walked reluctantly to the mirror.

"Yes, I am you and you are me. That is the face I remember. It's the face from the only childhood photo I possess of myself."

"Where was the photo taken?"

"At the front of the house."

"Oh my goodness! Do you mean the one of me standing by father's car?"

"Yes, that's right. I still have that photo. You will still have it when you are sixty-three."

Nick went weak at the knees and had to sit down. "So it's all true."

"Yes, I'm afraid so. Although I can hardly bear to say it, that's how it seems."

"Do you know, mother took that photo just three weeks ago."

"Yes I remember," smiled Nicholas. "She'd just taken one of Jeremy, and she was on her way back inside when I asked her if she would take one of me which she grudgingly agreed to."

"No, *I* asked her," said Nick with a grin.

"By the way, Nick. How old *are* you?"

"I'm thirteen."

"Yes, I thought that was about when the photo was taken. Well, perhaps you should get dressed now. We can't put off going down to dear mother any longer."

Nick was very scared. 'I'm going mad,' he thought. 'Hearing voices is definitely a bad sign of madness. What can I do? What's going to happen to me? I wish I knew someone who could tell me what to do. But I daren't tell anyone – I'd get locked up in the loony bin. But perhaps I don't need help, perhaps Nicholas really is who he says he is. After all, he knew all about the photo mother took of me; he knew that mother took it just after taking one of Jeremy. I don't see how he could possibly have known that if he isn't who he says he is. It's all such a nightmare. But it's *not* a nightmare. I wish it was; then it would all go away. Please tell me what to do, someone.'

# Chapter 3

"What sort of time do you call this? I hope you don't expect any breakfast."

Nick didn't seem to hear his mother and stood gazing out of the window.

"Listen to me when I am talking to you Nick. You're too late for breakfast, although there is a slice of cold toast left on the table which you can have."

"Yes mother," Nick said in a dreamy way.

"What's wrong with you? You look as if you have seen a ghost."

"I....er....Oh nothing! It was just a bad dream."

"Well, pull yourself together boy; we all have bad dreams sometimes. Get over it. And buck up if you want that toast. I have a lot to do today and I want you out of the house."

"Yes mother. Can I take a picnic lunch with me?"

"Certainly not. I haven't got time for all that. I'll give you some money to buy something for lunch. And I don't want to see you back in the house before six o'clock this evening."

Nicholas was scared. 'What the hell is happening to me?' he thought. 'Am I just imagining everything? Am I going mad? Perhaps this impossible thing is really happening. I don't have a body any more. I must have died, but my mind is somehow surviving inside Nick's head. I wonder if anyone has discovered my body at Poynings yet. It's horrible having to share someone else's mind, even if it is really mine in a way. But it isn't really mine. I'm not the same person as Nick; I have changed so much in fifty years. Everyone does, even after ten years or so. I feel completely helpless. I haven't the slightest idea how I can get out of this nightmare.'

§

Nick was delighted to escape from the house for a whole day. Normally he would be given jobs to do like cleaning the car or mowing the lawn. He had a plan for what he would like to do, but he did not want to tell Nicholas yet as he might not agree. But he would need some money for bus fares as well as what mother had given him. He did a paper round on Sundays and this earned him some money which he saved in a tin in his bedroom cupboard. He went upstairs to get the bus fare money from that.

When he had shut the bedroom door he spoke out loud.

"Nicholas, did you hear what mother said about having to go out all day?"

"Of course I did. I can hear everything you hear."

"Well, would you mind if I went to see your house at Poynings?"

"That's fine by me. But it seems a very strange thing for you to want to do."

"I'd like to see the house where I will end up living."

"OK. We can combine that with what *I* want to do, which is for us to walk there, and come back by bus."

"Walk!" Nick was horrified. "That's a hell of a distance to walk."

"No, it's only about 11 miles, and we'll be walking right along the ridge of the downs. It's a beautiful day and we can buy a picnic lunch at the baker's to take with us. You are a fit and strong boy; you're going to become very good at sports at your next school. It will be good training for you."

"OK. But when we get outside I want to try something out."

"What are you doing up there, Nick?" shouted mother from downstairs. "Come down at once. I want you out of the house now."

Nick grabbed his rucksack and some money from his tin and ran downstairs.

"Sorry mother. We're going now."

"What do you mean 'we'? Who are you going to be with? You know you have to tell me who you associate with. I won't have you hob-nobbing with riff-raff. It lets the family down."

"I'm not going with anyone, mother. I meant '*I'm*' going now."

She gave him a puzzled and suspicious look as they walked out to the road. As soon as they were clear of the house, Nick stopped and said, "Right, I want to do an experiment Nicholas. You try to stay standing still and I will try to walk along the pavement. Are you ready?"

"Yes," said Nicholas and he tried to keep his feet firmly on the ground. Nick strode down the pavement with a delighted grin on his face. He stopped. "OK," he said. "Let's try it the other way round now. You try and walk." Nicholas tried to step forward, but nothing happened. "There you are then. That means I'm the boss," said Nick.

"It simply means that it's your mind that I am occupying – temporarily I profoundly hope."

Just then Mrs Parsons, from two houses along from Nick's house, walked past. She stopped and gave Nick a very peculiar look and tried to find who he was talking to. "Oh dear Nick. Talking to yourself now, are you? Whatever next?" She walked on, shaking her head.

"Oh Lord!" said Nick. "That will certainly get straight back to mother and father."

"We must be much more careful about when we talk to each other. Not another word until we get on the downs. All right?" Nicholas wondered how he had got into this awful mess.

Ten minutes later, having called in at the baker's on the way, they were setting off along the footpath that ran behind Lewes Gaol. Soon they were climbing up a gentle slope on open downland. It was a beautiful summer day filled with the sound of larks beneath a dome of blue. Nicholas always found the familiar smell of chalk downs intoxicating.

After about 40 minutes walking they reached a point where the path levelled out for a while. Nicholas said, "I just want to leave the path to go to the top of that little hill on the right. The hill is called Blackcap." It was only a short distance to the top.

"What's this concrete block here for?" Nick asked.

"It's called a trig point, short for triangulation point. You will often find them at the tops of hills. They enable surveyors to make maps. The idea is that, in clear weather, you can see at least two other trig points. Using theodolites which have built-in telescopes surveyors can measure very accurately the angle between one of the distant trig points and the other. This enables them to make very accurate maps."

Nick was delighted with the views. "Can you tell me about the various things we can see from here?"

Nicholas pointed. "Looking to the east you can see Cuckmere Haven and the Seven Sisters."

"Oh yes, I've heard of the Seven Sisters. That's where the cliff goes up and down seven times in a row, isn't it?"

"That's right. That makes a wonderful walk too, but a bit more strenuous than this one. Cuckmere Haven is the low point at this end of the Sisters where the River Cuckmere flows out into the sea. I think I can just make out the river there. Now if you look to the north you can see a huge stretch of the Weald spread out. The Weald is the area of relatively low land between the North and South Downs."

"I've been to the top of Lewes Castle several times and there is a great view from there. But it's nothing like as good as this. This is amazing," enthused Nick. "Aren't we lucky that it isn't a misty day?"

"We are indeed. Now let's have a sit-down here for a short while. We still have some important talking to do."

"I know. After Mrs Parsons has talked to mother – which she certainly will do – we're going to be in deep shit."

"We'll just have to deal with that when it happens. But it highlights the importance of what I think we have to talk about now. You said this morning that you wanted to see my Poynings house, and when I asked you why, you said, 'I'd like to see the house where I will end up living.' I have to warn you that you may not end up living there. This is because I, or my conscious self, seem to have travelled back in time, and this has inevitably changed events. For example, when I was your age – when I was you – my 63 year-old self did *not* enter my mind. As a direct result of that I did not set out to walk to Poynings; after all, I didn't have a reason to – I didn't know I was going to live there in my retirement. It is universally accepted by scientists and others that it would be impossible to travel back in time. The classic example that is often quoted in support of this is that if someone travelled back in time to kill his own grandfather when a child, he could not do so because if he killed his grandfather before his father or mother had been conceived, he himself would not exist."

"Oh yes, I know about that. It's called the time paradox. I've just read a new book by Isaac Asimov called *The End of Eternity*. In the story it dealt with all the problems of time travel. I loved it."

"That will be very helpful now that you are part of it. You know, then, that the time travellers in the book tried to make changes in the past which would dramatically improve some situation or problem in the future. But they had always to make the smallest possible change needed to produce the wanted result. Otherwise the change would be likely to produce a great many other outcomes as well; these could often be bad or even disastrous.

"Despite the universal agreement of the scientists, *we* have proved that time travel into the past is *not* impossible, at least for minds if not bodies. This means that we have got to be very careful to make the changes we make as small as possible. We will inevitably make some changes. We are making one now – if it were not for what has happened to us, you wouldn't be walking on the downs now. I don't see how that change can make any significant alterations to the future, but I don't *know* this. The problem, I think, is that it is very difficult to see what sort of change could cause havoc in the future; it is hard to see 'the now' through the eyes of the future. But I think the fewer the people who know what has happened; the less likely it will be that big changes are made. At the moment it's just you and me and I think we should keep it that way for as long as possible."

"Yes I think I understand that. Blimey, I'm learning a lot today."

"Good. I think we should get walking again now."

They walked down from the top of Blackcap to rejoin the path. After a couple of minutes they came to a crossroads of paths and continued straight ahead.

"We have now joined the South Downs Way," said Nicholas. "It's a long-distance track running between Eastbourne and Winchester that has been used by travellers since Neolithic times as a dryer and safer route across this part of the country. We will be following it now along the ridge of the downs, for most of the way to Poynings"

After another forty minutes brisk walking they arrived at a minor road, crossed it and walked up a short slope to reach another trig point.

"This is the top of Ditchling Beacon, the highest point in East Sussex," said Nicholas.

"I think the views from here are even better than they were from Blackcap."

"I agree with you. You'll be relieved to hear that it is mostly downhill now from here to Poynings."

"Oh no, you're wrong. I love the climbing. There's a real sense of achievement."

"I'm so glad, Nick. Let's just carry on down the slope a bit to get out of the wind and then we can stop for our picnic lunch."

They soon found a sheltered spot, and Nick took off his rucksack and unpacked their lunch.

"I've been wondering if we can find another way of talking to each other which doesn't involve me talking out loud," said Nick "Have you any ideas?"

"Well, as a starter, try thinking hard about a single word – any word – and I will see if I can 'hear' you and tell you what the word is."

"Right, I'll do that. Erm…..OK, what's my word?"

Nicholas concentrated. "I'm getting something……I'm not sure……It sounds like 'haggle'."

"That's amazing. You're very close really. I was thinking of 'apple'."

"I think that has to be more than a coincidence. Now you try to hear the word I'm thinking of." Nicholas fiercely thought of a word.

"Well I think I could hear that all right. It was 'turnip' wasn't it?"

"Yes. Well done Nick. You seem better than me at mind-reading."

"Not necessarily. You might be better than me at sending."

They continued in this way while eating their lunch, starting with single words and progressing to short sentences. Soon they found that they seemed to be able to communicate very well with each other silently.

"Perhaps we had better be on our way," said Nicholas as he stood up.

"Hey, wait a minute," said Nick. "I didn't stand up then, you did. I wasn't trying to stand at all."

"It seems as if our minds are beginning to blend with each other. I suppose that's really good news, given that I don't know of any way I can leave your head, even though we may both wish that to happen."

"Well actually, I'm not sure if I *do* want that to happen." Nick felt confused and embarrassed, and hastily continued, "Anyway, let's try another experiment. I'll stand still, and you see if you can walk. Perhaps it will work this time."

Nicholas tried to walk and saw his right foot move forward a little shakily. Then when he took the next step he somehow managed to fall over. Nick was only just able to stop himself from rolling down the hill. "Never mind," he said. "It started working. It's just a matter of practice. We'll try again when we are on level ground."

They continued their walk, and as they did so Nick decided to test out their new-found communication skills. Thinking in what he thought was a loud way, he said, "How much further is it to your house?"

"We're just over half way," replied Nicholas, also silently. "So I guess we have another five miles to go."

"I think we've got the hang of this silent talking business."

"Definitely. I believe our minds may be slowly merging. How do you feel about that?"

"I'm not sure really. I think it's probably good. I mean, I like you," Nick said shyly.

"That's very good. Everyone should learn to like themselves. It's something I totally failed to do in my former life."

Before long they could see two windmills side by side below them as they dropped down a hill. When they reached them Nick was sorry to see that they could not go inside them. They were obviously privately owned.

"They are called Jack and Jill. The owners live here and the mills are not open to the public. But in my time Jill will be bought by the local district council and restored to full working order making flour. It was.....will be open to the public on Sunday afternoons, and there will even be a refreshment bar. Jack was still privately owned. I can't cope with the hassle of using the right tense. But I'm sure you understand what I mean."

"Yes I do. Do you know I'm starting to feel as if I'm living in history. It feels weird"

"Yes, Nick. It is all very weird."

They continued their walk and in another fifty minutes they were in Poynings. Nicholas stopped. "I did that. I must have done. You didn't know where to stop."

"Well done! We're really making progress all round."

"That walk wasn't too bad, was it?"

"Oh no, Nicholas. I absolutely loved it and I want to do lots more walks on the downs."

Nicholas chuckled. "You're me all right," he said. "When I was a teenager I think I must have walked almost every inch of public footpath on the downs. So you see you would have found this delight anyway."

He pointed to a house named Newtimber Cottage. "That's my house, or will be." Nicholas was feeling almost queasy. Everything seemed weird to him. Here he was pointing out his house to his thirteen-year-old self, which someone from the past was living in. It all seemed like the 'stuff of madness'.

"I love the house. I'm not surprised I'm going to buy it. Thatched roofs are great; is there an attic underneath it?"

"Yes, but I only used it for storage. Have you seen enough? We ought to get our bus back home."

"I certainly haven't seen enough. I want to see every room inside. But I know I can't do that. So let's go."

Travelling back home in the bus they both sat in slightly weary silence, thinking their own thoughts. They both felt a need for this; they needed a respite from each other. Nicholas returned to speculating about exactly who or what he was. In some ways he felt like Nick's puppet. But he supposed that Nick might well feel that it was the other way about. More importantly, was he, Nicholas Harrison, alive? He desperately wanted to return to his own body and resume his blissful life in Poynings. But apart from not having the faintest idea how to do this, he assumed it must be impossible anyway. His mind had clearly left his body. A body cannot continue to live without a mind. He must have become a corpse which someone would discover in due course. There would be a post mortem and, perhaps a police investigation. Then he would probably be buried in Poynings graveyard. He felt very bleak. The neighbours would be able to tell the police his name, but beyond that nobody knew anything about him – a sad old recluse whose life had added up to nothing. He hadn't even made a will, although he had a large amount of money in savings. There had never seemed to be a point in making a will; there was no-one to leave his money to. Perhaps he would feature on the BBC's *Heir Hunters* programme. Oh God, that would mean that Jeremy would inherit it all.

Nick was wondering what on earth was happening to him. He thought that Nicholas must be who he said he was. But how could he be completely sure? What if he was just a voice in his head? Perhaps he was going mad. It wouldn't be very surprising considering what rubbish parents he had. Yes, he knew for sure that his parents were no good. He knew this from hearing his friends when they occasionally talked about their parents. They all sounded like such wonderful people who actually loved their children. If his parents were like that perhaps he could talk to them about what was happening to him, although he supposed he would probably still end up in the loony bin.

# Chapter 4

Soon after Franklin Harrison had returned home from work, the back door bell rang. Mildred went to the door to find Dorothy Parsons standing there. "Oh hallo Dorothy. Nice to see you. Come in; I've just made a pot of tea."

"I'm afraid you won't think it's so nice to see me when you hear what I have to tell you."

"Oh dear, that doesn't sound too good."

Franklin came into the room to get a cup of tea. "Oh, sorry," he said. "Am I interrupting?"

"No, not at all. In fact I think it would be best if you stayed and heard what it is I have to say," said Mrs Parsons

They all sat down round the kitchen table. Nick's older brother, Jeremy, who had been eavesdropping, had hurried in to join them.

Mrs Parsons sat upright in her chair and cleared her throat importantly. "I'm afraid it's about your dear little Nick."

"What's the little brat done now?" said Jeremy.

"Shh! don't interrupt, dear. Let's hear what Mrs Parsons has to say." Dorothy turned to Mrs Parsons with her long-suffering look on her face.

"I was walking up the road this morning when I saw dear Nick walking towards me. He was chatting away and I tried to see who he was talking to, but there was no one else there. As he came by I said, "Hello Nick dear. It looked as if you were talking to yourself there." He just looked at me almost as if he didn't recognise me. But he didn't deny that he had been talking to himself.

"Did you hear what it was he was saying?" asked Franklin.

"Not entirely! But I did hear him saying something about someone 'occupying his mind'."

"Thank you for going to all the trouble of telling us, Mrs Parsons. It is very kind of you to keep us informed of what that boy is doing," said Mildred.

"Huh! That little creep is completely bonkers if you ask me….I think he…."

"We didn't ask you," Franklin interrupted. "Please leave the room."

"Well I'm sorry to be the bearer of bad tidings, as I say. I know you two will have lots to talk about so I'll get out of your way."

When she had gone, Mildred said, "Oh Frankie, what is that boy going to do next? He's nothing but trouble. I truly don't know what we have done to deserve such a creature."

"Yes, he can certainly let the family down. But perhaps he can't help it. Perhaps he's ill."

"Well I would like you to give him a good talking to when he comes home."

"Yes of course Mildred. I will see if I can get this nonsense sorted out."

Nick got home at a quarter to seven. His mother pounced on him immediately. "What sort of time do you call this? I told you to be back at six o'clock."

"No mother. You said don't get back before six. This is not before six, so I am following your instructions."

"Any more of that sort of cheek and you will go to bed without any dinner. Your father wants to have a talk with you. He is in the sitting room."

He went in to the sitting room knowing what this was about. He had already decided what he was going to say.

"Sit down, Nick. Now, I believe you were heard talking to yourself. Is that right?"

"Someone should tell Mrs Parsons to keep her nose out of other people's business."

"Nick, please do not talk like that about you elders and betters. She said that she told us about it because she was very concerned about you."

"She said that did she?"

"The point is that we are all concerned about you. Talking to oneself is a sign of mental illness, and we don't want any of that in our family."

"Everybody talks to themselves at times. It means nothing at all. I've heard *you* do it."

"You most certainly have not. But it's not just the talking to yourself. You have been behaving very strangely today."

"In what way have I been strange?"

"Your mother tells me that you were very vague this morning, not concentrating on anything, just miles away."

"Sorry father."

Nick went up to his bedroom and Franklin went off to find Mildred.

"I've had a talk with him," Franklin said. "He admitted that he had been talking to himself, but didn't think this was anything to worry about. I pointed out that it wasn't just that, but the fact that he was frequently very vague and didn't seem to hear when people spoke to him. In fact, 'away with the fairies' as some would call it."

"Well, he's off to his new school next week. So perhaps they will be able to sort him out."

"Oh thank God for that. Yes, let's hope they do."

§

"That man is pathetic," said Nick angrily. "I doubt if he knows the first thing about psychology. Yet I suspect he is dead keen to have me pronounced insane. That way they would get rid of me to some asylum; it would suit them down to the ground."

"Oh come on, Nick. You're exaggerating. I agree that there is very little to be said for their parenting skills and I certainly don't think either of them has ever loved you/me/us. But I'm certain they do not want you to be put in an asylum. Think of the disgrace to the family."

Nick laughed out loud. "That's odd" he said. "I don't believe you *can* think laughter."

"I think we should talk a little more about this business of not making any changes which might alter the future in some significant way. There is a branch of physics called Chaos Theory which was first developed in the last century. This theory suggests that there are certain circumstances or systems where some very small change in one place can produce a very large change in another place and after a period of time. But these 'chaotic' conditions only exist in certain kinds of situation. One example is the earth's atmosphere. It is this that makes weather forecasting such a difficult and complex activity. Many years later – in fact in the nineteen-sixties, so it's going to happen soon – another scientist called Edward Lorenz gave an example of the effects that can be seen in a complex system. He said it was like a butterfly opening its wings in one place resulting several weeks later in a hurricane developing somewhere else. This example will become famous and will be called the Butterfly Effect. It is, of course, a very extreme illustration and, I would guess, vanishingly unlikely to happen. But it illustrates what undoubtedly is true – that a small change in the atmosphere can produce a large change in the weather in a few days' or weeks' time.

"Now in most times and places the butterfly effect does not happen. But chaos theory is far from being fully understood – even in the first part of the next century, where I come from. But it does suggest that in our situation we should always try to make the changes we make as small as possible."

"Wow! That's the longest lecture you have given me…… I'm only teasing; I understand what you are saying and certainly agree that we must change as little as possible."

"The day after tomorrow is Sunday and you've got your newspaper round to do. The day after that is your first day at your new school. So tomorrow is the last full day we've got. Would you like to do another walk?"

"I would love that, Nicholas."

"OK! So if mother and father agree I……"

"I couldn't care less if they agree or not. We're going."

# Chapter 5

"I have a suggestion for our walk today," said Nicholas. "I think it would be nice to do another stretch of the South Downs Way. What do you think?"

"Oh I'd love that. It sounds great?"

"But I have to warn you that this walk is a little longer than the walk to Poynings. That was about 11 miles; this would be nearer 13 or 14 miles and is much hillier."

"I love it! I love it!"

"Good! It's just as well that I got up nice and early this morning."

"It was me who did that!" said Nick indignantly.

"Ah! It must have been both of us. The walk will finish at Alfriston and we will need to get the bus back from there. Although it's all very well for me to decide to pay a bus fare. I don't have any money; it's impossible for me to have money."

"Nonsense! You do have money. It's in the tin in my cupboard."

"You're a kind boy." Nicholas was embarrassed. It seemed ridiculous to be telling himself that he was kind. But he meant it.

When they went downstairs their mother was already up. She was always an early riser. Their father was having his usual Saturday lie-in. As they came into the kitchen she said, "My goodness! What are you doing up at half past six? It's unheard of."

"I know," said Nick. "But we are going for a long walk on the downs."

"Once again, you are failing to tell me who you are associating with. I won't have it."

"No I'm not. I mean I will be walking on my own."

"But you clearly said, '*we* are going for a walk'."

"I know. I'm not sure why. I think it must be my imaginary friend…..Max. I often think about him."

"For God's sake! Whatever next! I really think we are going to have to send you away for treatment if this kind of rubbish continues. You're growing up. You're not a child of five any more. Where are you going to walk?"

"To Alfriston," said Nick, "and then I'll get a bus back."

"I expect you'll be wanting to take a picnic. There's bread in the bin, and bits and pieces in the fridge. Help yourself."

"Thank you mother," said Nick, astonished.

§

They walked to Southover High Street and then along Juggs Road. This led on to a pleasant footpath which took them through the village of Kingston and up the steep side of Castle Hill. Where the steep part of the climb finished, Nicholas said, "This is where we join the South Downs Way." He pointed to a well-worn path which crossed the one they were on a little way ahead. They continued to the highest point of the hill. They could see the whole of Lewes spread out below them. They quickly found the road where they lived, although they weren't sure that they could pick out the individual house.

As they walked on, Nick said, "I've been thinking…..about thinking. We can hear each other inside my head when we're talking to each other. But I don't think we each know what the other is thinking, do we? Certainly I never know what you're thinking."

"It's the same for me. It is odd, I suppose. And yet, you know, if we could 'hear' each other's thoughts all of the time, it would be awful. Just imagine! It would be like two people talking to us, one at each ear, all the time, without ever a break. I don't think we could stand that; we certainly would go mad then. So it's just as well we don't do this."

"Do you think it's just a matter of luck that we can't hear each other think?" asked Nick.

"Gosh! You do ask difficult questions, don't you? First, you must remember that I don't *know* anything about any of this. I expect you know that the human brain is split into two halves. There are plenty of connections between the two halves, but not every part of one half is directly connected to every part of the other. My guess is that since I 'moved in' we have each been occupying just one half of your brain. And I also guess that the two areas which we use for thinking have not been directly connected to each other. Of course we can choose to tell each other about what we are thinking, as I am now, but this is not through a direct connection; we have to use the new connection we have made for ourselves that allows us to talk to each other without speaking out loud. I would make an even bigger guess that, just as our two brain-halves have made a choice about the speaking connection, so they have also made a choice about *not* connecting the 'thinking' areas of each half. This may all be complete garbage. But even if we had a spare neurologist handy, I don't think he or she would be able to give us any answers either. Neurologists would have had no experience of our situation, I would assume. What do you think?"

"Yes, that all seems to fit with how it.....I don't know......how it sort of *feels* to me."

When they had walked up and down the other side of two more hills they reached the small village of Southease. They then soon arrived at a bridge over a river.

"This is the River Ouse. It's the same river that flows through Lewes. It enters the sea just south of here at Newhaven. We are now nearly half-way along our planned walk. How are you? If you've had enough we will shortly reach Southease Halt on the railway line from Newhaven to Lewes and we could get a train home from there."

"No I'm fine. I'd hate not to do the whole walk."

"That was a silly question for me to ask, really. I knew you weren't feeling weary because your muscles are my muscles."

"You do use some funny words."

"What?"

"'Weary'. Nobody uses 'weary' any more, do they? It's straight out of the school hymn book."

"Well I do."

They walked on, soon passing Southease Halt and crossing a main line. Then they started climbing yet another steep hill.

"You know," said Nicholas, "there is another part of my brain that you can't 'read', or I don't think you can. You can't reach my memories, can you?"

There was a short pause while Nick tried to find any of Nicholas's memories. "No I can't. Or, at least, if I can I don't know how to do it."

"Of course, I can always tell you anything from my memory which you would like to know about. After all, they are memories of a life that will presumably be your life, perhaps with a few exceptions, but I hope with a lot. So always feel free to ask."

"Thank you Nicholas. I will."

Having reached the top of the hill they were now on another stretch of downland ridge which was more or less level. At the end of the ridge the path followed a short gradient up to the top of another hill.

"We're now at the top of Firle Beacon, another wonderful spot for views. If you look that way towards the North West you can see the little village of Firle and beyond that on the other side of the main road and the railway there is another village called Glynde. Just to the left of Glynde you can see another of the well-known high points of the Sussex Downs, Mount Caburn. Look a little to the left of Caburn and in the far distance you can see Lewes."

"Wow! It's amazing to think that we have walked that far."

When they had feasted themselves on the fantastic views they walked on along the South Downs Way for a short distance, reaching a picnic site beside a car park at the top of a narrow lane which came to a dead end here. They stopped here to have their lunch.

"The very steep little lane that ends just here is called Bopeep Hill," said Nicholas. "It is named after Bopeep Farm which is in the valley below. I believe they hold hill climbing competitions up this lane, sometimes for vintage cars and sometimes for motor bikes."

When they had finished their lunch they soon reached the top of another hill. Nicholas pointed, "There you are, that's the village of Alfriston below, where we finish our walk."

"What?" said Nick, looking at his watch. "Already! It's only half past one."

"Yes, but remember we set out at eight o'clock. We've been walking for five and a half hours."

"And it's been absolutely wonderful again. You make it even better with your explanations about what we are looking at."

"Thank you, Nick. I'm delighted you feel that way."

They were soon in Alfriston. They were lucky that they only had to wait twenty minutes for their bus back to Lewes.

When they got back home, Franklin said, "Mother said you were out walking on the downs. You haven't really walked all the way to Alfriston, have you?"

"Yes I have," said Nick proudly.

"Well I'm blowed!"

# Chapter 6

Nick was setting out from the newsagents to do his paper round.

"Do you need to concentrate on what you're doing when you do this paper round?"

"Heavens, no! I could do it in my sleep."

"That's good, because there are some serious things we need to talk about. It's what someone I used to know would call a DMC – a Deep, Meaningful Conversation."

"You mean it's not.....an SDT?"

"What's that?"

"A short, dirty talk!"

Nicholas burst out laughing. An older boy across the road glared at Nick. "What are you laughing at?"

"Sorry I was just laughing at something I was thinking about."

The older boy looked as if he might just give Nick the benefit of the doubt.

"I need to tell you a few things about my life – the life that *might* become yours. It's not been a very happy life, and that's for one very basic reason. I have learned to hate and despise myself and I have never learned how to like other people and enjoy their company. You are leading that same life, and I think that it is desperately important that you learn how to change it into a loving and sociable life. I can't bear to think of you repeating the same miserable journey that I made. Now I know that we have talked about the need to be careful about making changes. But I really can't imagine that you learning to become a normal person is going to flap too many butterflies' wings.

"I remember clearly that you have not had any of these problems so far. You and I made some good friends at Motcombe School as well as doing very well in our school work. OK so far?"

"Yes. It sounds as if it's going to be a very sad story. But please carry on."

"I suppose it's not too surprising that I grew, through my teenage years, to become a person without love in my heart, without compassion, without any caring instinct and without interest in people. I had been taught that this was the right way to be by Mother, Father and Jeremy. A while after I began at Denport Abbey School I started to find that almost everyone was either too stupid or too irritating for me to want to have anything to do with them.

"I am saying 'I' rather than 'you' because for me, all that I have said above is unalterably true. But none of it has to be true for you if you choose for it not to be so, and if you work very hard at combating the influences of your family.

"I think I have said enough for now – I suspect that you may already have put a few newspapers through the wrong letter boxes. I would like to hear what you think about what I have said. But later, not now. That way everyone else may get the right newspapers, and also you will have time to think about what I have said. We will have bags of time to talk some more on the long train journey to Denport Abbey school tomorrow."

§

The next morning Nick found himself with nothing much to do before ten o'clock when he and Jeremy were due to set out on their journey to school. His trunk, packed with all his clothes, had been collected with Jeremy's by British Railways on Saturday to be taken to the school using the Passengers' Luggage in Advance system. What a good system that was, thought Nicholas, and what a shame it would be discontinued at some time in the 1960s.

Nick and Nicholas were sitting in the kitchen continuing where they had left off the previous day.

"Have you given some thought to what I was telling you about yesterday?"

"Yes, I've thought about it a lot. I feel very sad for you Nicholas. I can't imagine what it must be like to have been through a long life and know that, at the end of it, you have no real friends. And, of course, it scares me like hell because it looks as if that has to be what lies ahead for me."

"I believe you are wrong there. I am convinced that you can change the way you are."

"But that isn't the way I am. I can't see what there is for me to change. I don't dislike people – well apart from Jeremy. How can I change from being what I'm not, if you see what I mean?"

"Yes, Nick, I understand that. I should have said, '….change the way you will be."

Nick felt his shoulder being shaken hard. "Nicholas, Nicholas, will you pay attention when I'm talking to you?" Jeremy was looking on with a sneer.

"What on earth is wrong with you boy? You were in a dream; it was almost as if you had been hypnotised."

"I'm sorry, mother. I don't know what happened. I suppose I couldn't hear you."

"But you're not deaf." She lowered her voice to a whisper, "You can hear me now, can't you?"

"Yes, mother," said Nick miserably.

"You just don't take any notice of me. You seem to be able to switch off your attention. I hope you don't do this to other people."

"Oh, yes he does." interrupted Jeremy. "He's done it to me several times in the last few days. He just blanks out."

"Well, it had better not happen at school or they will be sending you home again. Then what will I be able to do with you?"

"No more talking for now, Nick. I hadn't realised that was happening."

"Nor had I," said Nick.

§

When they got on the train at Brighton station Jeremy said to Nick, "You sit there. I'm going up the other end of the carriage. But do not get off the train until I tell you."

"I know we need to change at Victoria, I'm not a fool."

"That's your opinion, worm," said Jeremy, and he went up to the far end of the carriage.

"Thank goodness he's gone," said Nick. "Are you ready to carry on from where we left off?"

"Yes. I was saying that neither you nor I have or had any of the relationship problems that I was talking about at this point in our lives. But I was saying that it was after I started at Denport Abbey that it all began. I can only assume that it is about to start for you, unless you take steps to avoid it."

"But I don't know what I have to do."

"Of course you don't. But I think I can help you with this. I know that may surprise you. You're probably thinking that I am completely unfit to help you.

"Let me explain. When I retired I had all the time in the world to look back at my life and wonder about my inability to relate to other people. I decided to do some research in psychological writings and it soon became apparent that I had been seriously damaged by my parents. However the cause of my problems didn't really matter, especially as I had already more or less worked that out for myself. What I needed was to discover how to change things, to learn how to make good connections with other people. I had to forget everything I had learned and assumed on the subject up to then, and replace these ideas and feelings with some basic principles of good relationships. I was able to discover what these principles were from my reading. I had already started to put them into practice, with a certain degree of success, before I was whisked away into your head. I believe that I can now pass these principles on to you so that you can use them to develop really good friends at school. Friends you feel you can trust and who feel they can trust you. What do you think?"

"Well, I don't actually....."

Once again Nick felt his shoulder being shaken. This time it was the ticket inspector wanting to see his ticket. "Are you all right?" the inspector said.

"Oh, yes. I'm sorry. I'm fine."

"You were miles away. I asked you for your ticket several times, but you just continued to stare straight ahead as if you were seeing a ghost."

"I'm really sorry. I didn't mean to be rude." He took his ticket out of his pocket and passed it over.

They soon arrived at Victoria station. They travelled on the Circle Line to Liverpool Street. Before going up into the main line station, Jeremy pulled Nick to one side. "From here on," he said, "we are likely to see boys from the school including some of my friends...."

"I don't believe it; you've actually got some friends at the school?"

Jeremy kicked him on the shins. "So from now on you stay well away from me. When we are at school you will *never* speak to me. You are nothing to do with me at all. Do you understand?"

"Don't you think that even your bird-brained friends would find the name Harrison a little bit of a clue?" This time Nick dodged Jeremy's foot. "Anyway it all suits me fine. I won't want any of my friends to know that *you* are *my* brother."

# Chapter 7

"Here we are," said Nicholas as the train pulled in to Grantham station. A flock of boys filled the platform. "There will be a bus waiting outside the station."

Nick followed all the other boys on to the waiting bus. The boy sitting next to Nick seemed a lot older than him. He had thought of trying to make friends with whoever sat next to him, but he now felt that this would not be a good plan. Never mind, he could talk to Nicholas instead. Then he thought better of that too. Supposing another boy spoke to him. He would blank him out. That would not be a good start to Nicholas's plan to make him Mr Popular. After half an hour travelling on the bus it turned into a long driveway at the end of which was a huge old house.

Just inside the main entrance to the school building was a large sign saying, "*Will all the new first year boys please come to the main theatre at 6:00 sharp.*"

"It's just gone four now, so that gives us plenty of time for me to give you a quick tour of the school."

"OK, but please keep what you say to short comments with lots of space between. I'm really worried about the blanking out problem."

"Yes, of course," said Nicholas.

He started by walking round the outside of the main building. He pointed out the numerous modern buildings that had been added. They could be identified by signs outside each building, indicating that they were used for particular subjects. There were buildings for music, science, drama and physical education. There was also a very large building which was open. They went inside to find a two-tiered auditorium and a stage. "This is used for plays, films, school assemblies, and other meetings – such as ours at six o'clock."

Nick already knew that the school grounds were massive from the twenty minutes that it had taken the bus to travel from the main gate to the school building. Apart from the large area set aside for games fields, the rest seemed to be almost entirely woodland. He was beginning to like the place already.

"Where's the swimming pool. Is it in one of these buildings?"

"Oh no! The swimming pool here is the river."

"Yugh! The river's full of mud and slimy things isn't it?"

"Not at all. It's great. There are diving boards and steps for getting out. You have to pass a test before you can use the bathing place. You have to swim across the river and back with clothes on. Two of the boys who have got their life-saver qualifications have to go across with you. I passed the test first time, so I expect you will."

"Yes, I think I should be able to."

Nicholas took Nick in to look round the inside of the main building. They saw all sorts of rooms for doing school work in and a rather boring-looking library. When they went down to the basement floor, Nicholas pointed out what he called the tuck shop. It appeared to be a sort of café. "You can buy snacks and drinks there in the breaks between lessons if you want to."

"But I don't have any money. I left my tin of savings at home."

"Don't worry; you can get some pocket money every week from your housemaster. It's all part of the school fees bill which father has to pay."

"Oh I like that," said Nick.

All the dormitories were on the first floor. The part that Nick most enjoyed, though, was the huge area of attic space.

Much of this had been divided up into studies. Depending on the size of each study, it was used by two, three or four boys. But for Nick the best thing of all was a model railway club. When they got there they found that it was open with existing members hoping to sign up new first year boys. Nick thought it was amazing. There was a huge layout in this large attic room, all electrified, with six stations and goods yards and landscape and tunnels and signals and lots of trains which were controlled by equipment located at each of the stations. When he found that there was no membership fee, Nick signed up straight away. He was told that the whole layout – the track, the landscape, even the trains – had been built by many boys over the years, and things were still being improved and added to even now.

At five to six Nick walked into the school theatre for the meeting of first year boys. There were seventy or eighty boys of his own age in the auditorium, all chattering away to each other. For the first time since arriving at the school, Nick felt rather overwhelmed. The thought of having to make friends with all these other boys seemed too much to cope with and he said so to Nicholas.

"Don't worry Nick. You don't have to be friends with all of them; you just need to learn not to *dis*like any of them too much. I can help you with this. Not now, though. Later when we are on our own."

Just then, a man walked on to the stage and stood by a lectern that had been placed in the centre. "Good afternoon boys. My name is Mr Bullen and I am your housemaster," he said.

A number of the boys chorused, "Good afternoon Mr Bullen."

"Thank you for your greeting. I know you have been taught to do that at other schools. But, and here's the first of many things you are going to learn about Denport Abbey, we don't do that here. We believe that anything said in chorus is done on autopilot, and is therefore almost certainly not sincere.

"On your way out of here you will find on a table in the foyer a lot of envelopes, each one with one of your names on it. You will find that your envelope contains all the information you will need to be able to know and understand not only the school rules, but also all the many other things you need to know in order to settle quickly into the school routine. Among the items the envelope contains are maps of each floor of the main building labelled to show where all the rooms you need to know about are located, and a timetable to show you when and where all your lessons take place.

"But first I would like to tell you a few of the basics. The whole school is divided into six houses – Grantham, Lincoln, Spalding, Boston and Gainsborough. In addition there is Junior house, which is the one all of you will belong to. After your first year, you will be moved to one of the other five houses to which you will continue to belong for the rest of you career at this school.

"You have all been placed into sets for each of the main subject areas, in accord with your results in the entrance exams. These sets are numbered 1, 2 and 3, 1 being the top set. Your class label also includes a letter – A to E to show the year group. You first year boys will all be in classes starting with an E. You may well find that you are in E1 for maths and E2 for English for example, again according to your exam results.

"Those are the basics; all the rest is in your envelope. I strongly recommend that you spend the rest of today studying its contents. You can do this in the junior house common room, or, if you would like somewhere quieter there's the library. When you have all got an envelope you will find two prefects waiting for you in the foyer. They will show you the way to the dining hall for your evening meal which is at 6:45."

# Chapter 8

After a delicious meal of bangers and mash, Nick made his way to the library to look through the contents of his envelope. He was very impressed. It was detailed and clear. He only once had to ask Nicholas for an explanation of something. Otherwise he felt he knew everything there was to know about the school.

"What time do we have to go to bed?" Nick asked Nicholas.

"First years have to be in bed by nine o'clock, I think. But you have to unpack your trunk before that."

"Oh yes! I'd forgotten about that. I'll go and do it now."

By the time he had unpacked, had a wash and got into bed the other boys started to arrive. They shyly introduced themselves to each other and exchanged their first impressions of the school. The boy in the bed next to Nick's was called Martin.

"What set are you in?" asked Martin

"I'm in 1."

"What, for everything?"

"Yes"

"You must be a boffin. How boring!" said Martin.

"Is it? Why do you think that's boring?"

Martin now felt sorry he had said it. "Oh, I don't know. I suppose I expect I wouldn't understand anything you talk about."

Nick was irritated by this. Then he realised that this was what Nicholas had warned that he might feel about everyone. He was determined not to do that, starting now. "What clubs are you interested in joining?" he asked Martin.

"There's a fantastic model railway club. I've already joined it."

"So have I. It looks brilliant."

"I couldn't find where the swimming pool is on any of the maps. Hasn't the school got one?"

"Apparently we use the river."

"Wow! That's brilliant."

They continued to chat to each other until the lights were put out at 9:00.

"Right," said Nick to Nicholas, "now we can talk without worrying about whether we are blanking anyone out."

"Yes. It sounded as if you weren't having any problems getting on with Martin."

"Well, he really irritated me when he said that thing about being a boffin. But I then thought that this was the kind of thing I've got to work on. So I just put that remark out of my mind. And actually I like the chap; we seem to be interested in some of the same things."

"That's wonderful. Well done! One of the things that can help a lot when you come across someone who irritates you is to think about why he is doing or saying whatever it is that irritates. Have you any ideas about why Martin said that about being a boffin?"

"Well, I suppose he might have had hard times with people he thought were....I don't know....cleverer than him."

"So what do you think you can do to help him to deal with this?"

"Well certainly, I think, to do what I did – just put the remark out of my mind. And then help him to realise that kids in Set 1 aren't necessarily snooty."

"Yes, and you did that too. You helped him to discover that you were both interested in some of the same things."

"Thank you Nicholas. I'm determined not follow in your footsteps in relating to other people. Oh, God! I'm sorry. That was very rude."

"That's not being rude; I'm delighted to hear you say it. Now, if you don't mind, I'm tired and would like to get some sleep. I'm not sure I'm allowed to get tired; I'm just a mind."

"Minds can get tired. Goodnight."

§

The next day school started in earnest. Nick had English in the first period. The teacher was Mr Crimble. He said that in the first three lessons of the term he was going to teach them about 'parts of speech'. He asked the class what this phrase meant. Nick didn't know. One boy put his hand up. He said, "It is the grouping of words into different types, like adjectives, nouns and so on."

"Did you know that, Nick?" asked Nicholas.

"No, but I do now. Mr Crimble seems like a nice guy."

"It's a bit early to…."

They were interrupted by a piece of chalk hitting Nick's head. His attention was jolted back to Mr Crimble.

"What is your name, young man?"

"Nick Harrison, sir."

"Well Mr Harrison, I asked you a question, but you seemed to have fallen into a trance." The class giggled. "I asked you what type of word 'quickly' is."

"Oh, it's an adverb, sir."

"Quite right. Well done. Are you the brother of Jeremy Harrison in the fourth year? You look very alike."

Nick hesitated. "No sir."

At the end of the lesson Mr Crimble said, "Your assignment for this week is to write an essay entitled 'My First Impressions of Denport Abbey'. If you ever forget what the assignment for any week is, you can find it on the assignments notice board in the main corridor. The same applies to all your subjects."

The school day was divided up into lessons and study time. The assignments for all subjects had to be completed in study time and handed in at the first lesson for each subject in the following week. The afternoons from 2:00 till 4:00 each week were for sports. Each boy was allocated one afternoon of 'free time' when they could do whatever they wanted. Tuesday and Thursday evenings from 7:00 till 8:00 were additional study times, called Prep, to work on assignments. Saturday afternoons and Sundays after school assembly were free time.

All in all a pretty hectic schedule Nick thought at the end of the first full week. He was struggling to complete all the assignments in time, but he was managing to do it by using some of his free time as well. He was determined to do well in his school work. You never knew, mother and father might actually feel proud of him, but he doubted it.

"I would like to go swimming this afternoon. Will there be the necessary people there for me to pass my test, Nicholas?"

"I don't know. But I would have thought so. There must be a lot of first years wanting to pass their test."

"Let's go down to the river anyway and see."

When they got there they found the swimming area crowded, mostly with first years eager to take their test. There were two teachers and several lifesavers – older boys who had been trained in lifesaving techniques and passed a tough test. One of the teachers was Mr Troy, who taught Nick's geometry class. The other one Nick hadn't seen before.

There was already a boy in the water wearing his games clothes doing the test. There was a lifesaver swimming beside him and another rowing a dinghy. They had just turned round at the other side of the river, which was about twenty metres across, Nick thought. Suddenly the boy taking the test seemed to get into trouble; he was gasping for breath with a lot of thrashing of water. He shouted, "Help me!" and the life saver in the water swam to him – he was only one stroke away. The drowning boy reached out and clutched the lifesaver round his neck. For a moment they both went under, but they soon reappeared with the boy still clutching the lifesaver fiercely round his neck. Nick felt very scared; it looked as if things were going badly wrong. The lifesaver pushed up and out on the boy's chin with the ball of his hand while pulling the boy towards him with his other hand at the bottom of his back. The drowning boy was pushed over backwards breaking his grip on the lifesaver and went under the water. The lifesaver followed and they both reappeared with the first year on his back being held firmly by the lifesaver's hands either side of the boy's head. He pulled the boy back to the bank using the backstroke leg motion to move through the water. Two other lifesavers on the bank helped the boy up the ladder coughing, spluttering and shaking like a leaf.

Nick was filled with astonishment and admiration at what he had just seen. The lifesaver in the water climbed the ladder and moved away a little to sit on the grass. Nick went over to him and sat down. "Gosh, that was incredible. I've never seen anything so wonderful. It must be so hard to do. What's your name?"

"Graham Whistler. I'm a fourth year. What's yours?"

"Nick Harrison."

"Well Nick, no, it's not particularly difficult once you've been trained."

"How does it feel to know that you've just saved someone's life?"

"It feels very good, no doubt about it. I suppose it was one of the reasons I chose to take the training. And, of course, being regarded as a hero by people like yourself who haven't seen it before is pretty damned good, too," he said, grinning.

Nick suddenly felt very embarrassed, and his face went red.

"Hey!" said Graham. "Don't be embarrassed. You've made my day. Really. I tell you what. It sounds as if you should do the training. You're allowed to apply when you move into the third year."

"I definitely will. What happened in the river just now when you seemed to push the boy under the water?"

"It's called a 'release'. It's the first thing you have to do if the swimmer holds on to you. If you don't do that then you will both drown. Learning the various releases is an important part of the training. There are different release techniques depending on how the swimmer catches hold of you. Of course, we always tell the people before they take the test that, if they get into trouble, they should roll on to their back, stretch out straight and put their head back so that their ears are just under the water. Actually, as we also always explain, if you do that you can't avoid floating.

"But it isn't too surprising that many people forget everything we have said in the panic of the moment when they think they are about to drown."

"Are you scared when you're doing it?"

"Yes, a bit. Actually, I think that's no bad thing when you think of the sheer size of the responsibility you are taking on. Anyway, it's my turn to do another stint now. Would you like to be the victim?"

"Yes please. But isn't there a queue?"

"Not really. Its first come, first served. So come on then. Let's go. Do you want to jump in or climb down the ladder?"

"I'll jump in."

"Now be careful, young Nick," said Nicholas. "Remember you're responsible for two of us."

"Shut up, Nicholas," said Nick, and he jumped in.

He used slow and strong strokes, remembering that there was no hurry. He was surprised that the water was nothing like as cold as he had thought it would be. When he got close to the opposite bank, Graham said, "OK! Turn round and swim back now."

When he had finished the swim and climbed on to the bank, Graham said, "Well done Nick. You're all right. You're a good swimmer. All the more reason for you to apply to train as a lifesaver when you're in the third year. By the way, are you anything to do with Jeremy Harrison."

"Absolutely not!" said Nick.

Graham looked at him curiously for a moment, and then grinned. "I quite understand. No-one wants to have much to do with Jeremy."

Nick looked worried. It seemed that he had let slip the secret. "Please don't tell him that you know I'm his brother. He told me that he would make life hard for me if I told anyone."

"Huh! Typical! Don't worry, I won't tell anyone."

"Thanks, Graham."

Nick changed into his normal clothes and sat down on the grass to watch the rest of the swimming tests. A boy still in games clothes sat down beside him. "Hi! I'm Tony Best. What's your name?"

"Nick Harrison."

"I saw you do your swimming test. You're a good swimmer."

"Thank you. Good luck with yours."

"Thanks. It won't be a problem; I've been swimming for years."

"That's good. What game have you chosen to do this year?"

"Football. I love football. How about you?"

"I've decided to do rowing, because I know nothing about it. It's completely new. I'm really glad I did; it's great. I think I'm beginning to get the hang of it."

At that moment a life saver came over to Tony and said, "Come on. It's time for your test."

Nick watched. He was swimming well. But when he had to turn round to come back, something went wrong and he was floundering and started shrieking at the top of his voice. He grabbed the life saver by his hair and they both went under. The life saver from the dinghy dived in and after a few seconds, which seemed to last for ever, all three appeared again. One of the life savers swam a few strokes to the boat and pulled it back. Tony frantically reached out for the boat and clung on. The life saver hauled himself into the boat, and then both of them man-handled Tony in. They rowed and swam back to the bank. Tony sat down, looking very miserable. Nick walked over to him.

"Are you alright," he said.

"Oh shut up! Leave me alone and mind your own business."

"I'm sorry. I was just worried about you. That looked like a horrible experience you had."

"Bugger off, will you?"

Nick walked away to the back of the swimming area. "What the hell was that all about, Nicholas? Why was he so nasty to me? What had I done to hurt him?"

"You hadn't done anything to hurt him. But what do you think he was feeling at that moment?"

Nick thought about this. "I expect he was feeling rather ashamed of his failure."

"Is there any reason that he should feel particularly ashamed in front of you?"

"Maybe because I had passed the test."

"And….?"

"I don't know….Well, he had just told me, before he did the test, that he was a good swimmer and wouldn't have a problem with it."

"Exactly so. And why do you think he had told you that?"

"I suppose because he wanted me to think he was a fit, sporty type and that he was very confident."

"That's right. And why do people sometimes want everyone to think that they are better, fitter, stronger, cleverer than most people?"

"I've no idea."

Nicholas said nothing and waited.

"Is it because they think that that way people will want to be friends with him, and he would then become popular instead of them thinking he wasn't very nice?"

"It could well be. And why do you think they might believe they are not very nice?"

"OK Nicholas, because they have been taught by their parents that they aren't very nice. But that's nonsense. I don't show off do I?"

"No you don't, because you haven't yet given way to that kind of despair. But remember, I have already travelled this journey, and according to that history, you are about to succumb. But you can stop it happening by knowing how these things work. By knowing that you are an admirable human being. By *choosing* to leave the legacy of your parents behind."

"I am really going to try to do that."

"Always remember that when you meet someone who is mean or nasty or bad-tempered or bullying or sarcastic or whatever, there is always a reason, something in their experience that has pushed them that way. It is *never* because they were born that way."

"You do...."

Nick was being shaken by the shoulder.

§

Mr Troy had been reluctant to take on the responsibility of supervising the swimming tests. But it was always rewarding to see kids achieving things. And actually the responsibility he had was nowhere near as great as that carried by the lifesavers.

What an admirable thing to do. But he thought it must be pretty scary.

He became aware of a commotion at the back of the swimming area. There was a crowd of boys doing a lot of shouting. He walked over pushing boys aside to get through. There, sitting by the fence, was the cause of the commotion. It was young Nick Harrison looking....looking what?....rather ghastly actually. His eyes were glassy, staring straight ahead of him; unseeing. He seemed like a statue, completely motionless.

He turned back to the crowd. Alright, move away please. Give us some room. He bent down and shook Nick by the shoulder. Instantly Nick looked up at him.

"What's up, Harrison? Are you alright?"

"Yes, sir. I'm fine."

"You were sitting there looking as if you were carved from marble."

"Oh, Lord! Was I? I was just thinking about something."

"Didn't you know there was a large crowd of boys standing round you shouting their heads off?"

"No sir, I'm afraid I didn't. I must have been lost in thought," he said.

"There are just two more swimming tests to be done, and then we are closing the swimming area for the day. I want you to come with me to see the school nurse."

"Oh, sir, there's no need for that. I'm absolutely fine."

"The nurse will be the best judge of that."

# Chapter 9

When they reached the medical centre Mr Troy told Nick to sit down in the waiting area. He knocked on the nurse's door and went in.

"Good afternoon Mrs Platten. I'm rather concerned about a first year called Nick Harrison. He's waiting outside. I was supervising at some swimming tests and became aware of a crowd of boys at the back making a lot of noise. When I went over to see what was going on, I found the boys were all standing round Nick who was sitting down by the fence. I looked at Nick, and I have to say that I have never seen anything like it. He was completely still with wide, empty, staring eyes. The boys were shouting to try to wake him up, I suppose. It made no difference at all. It seemed as if, as far as Nick was concerned, they didn't exist.

"He had been fine earlier and, indeed, had passed his swimming test with flying colours. But for no reason that I know of, he went into this trance-like state. Moreover, Mr Crimble was earlier telling me of a similar episode which Nick had in his English class."

"Right, let's have a look at him then."

Mr Troy ushered Nick in. "Would you like me to wait outside?"

"If you wouldn't mind, thank you."

Nick went into the surgery looking very miserable.

"I gather you're having some problems. Can you tell me about them?"

"I'm sorry, nurse, but I don't know anything about them."

"Do you know that every now and then you seem to go into a kind of trance, and during this trance you do not seem to be able to see or hear anything around you?"

"All I know is what people tell me. I have no experience....I mean I don't know that they happened. All I know is that on three or four occasions someone has told me that I have just had one of these....thingies."

"I know about two of them. When did the others happen?"

"Before term started." Nick felt that he was going to burst into tears at any moment. He must stop that happening.

"How long ago was the first time someone told you that it had happened?"

"About three weeks ago."

"You mean at home? Do your parents know about this?"

"Yes."

Nick mumbled this so quietly that Mrs Platten could hardly hear him. She could see that the poor boy was almost at the end of his tether; he was obviously at the edge of tears. "Nick I am sorry about all this. It must be horrible for you. I think we must get the doctor to take a look at you. I would like you to come here again on Monday at ten o'clock. I will give you a chit to say that you are excused lessons from ten till eleven on Monday."

§

It wasn't until lights out in the dormitory that evening that Nick and Nicholas felt it was safe for them to talk again. "It looks as if things are getting out of our control," said Nicholas.

"Yes, I know."

"There's nothing we can do about it. All we can do is to try to prepare for what will probably happen next."

"But we don't know what that will be, do we?"

"Well, I think it is quite likely that the doctor will want to refer us to a specialist. In 2013, where I come from, that would almost certainly involve having a brain scan so that a neurologist could look for clues and abnormalities in the brain. But scanners have not been invented yet. So I would think it would be most likely that we will be referred to some kind of psychotherapist."

"You keep saying 'we'. But as far as everyone else is concerned I am one thirteen-year-old boy."

"Yes, but so far as I am concerned we are two people, and I wanted to make it clear to you that I am entirely on the same side as you and will always be supporting you in every way I can."

"Thank you, Nicholas. I have a horrible feeling that I am soon going to need that support badly. I felt completely out of my depth when I was talking to the nurse."

"I know. But I thought you did extraordinarily well. If you are ever stuck for what to say to someone – the doctor, the therapist or anyone – just ask me, silently, to do the talking. The person we are talking to will not be able to tell the difference, naturally."

"That may well turn out to be a life-line. But I will always try to do the talking myself if I can. Is that alright with you?"

"I think that's very good, and exactly as it should be. I don't know about you, but I think one of the things that really weighs me down is the need to tell someone what has happened to us. It feels too big for just the two of us to carry. How do you feel about it?"

"I'm so glad you said that. I've been feeling exactly the same, and I've also been feeling guilty about wanting to tell someone, because I know it would be a very stupid thing to do....the shortest route to the loony bin, not to mention making bad changes to the future."

"I have been thinking about this, and it dawned on me that, theoretically, there is one way we could get someone to believe our story."

"That's fantastic. How can it be done?"

"Don't get too excited. It is, as I say, only theoretical. But it could be done if I could remember some major, headline-grabbing event that is shortly going to happen. I would need to be able to remember the exact date and a lot of surrounding details to the event."

"Yes, of course! That's a brilliant idea. If you told someone our story and then told them the date of the big event with all the details, then when it all turned out to be true, they would have no choice but to believe us."

"Quite so! But in the real world, people don't remember that sort of detail about anything which happened fifty years ago, let alone the exact date."

"Oh come on, Nicholas! Come on! Just think."

"I have been, Nick. Believe me, I have been. To give you an idea of how hard it is, can you tell me the date of any major event that occurred in 1960, just three years ago."

Nick thought about this for several minutes. Then he said, "No, I'm completely stumped."

"You see, and that was only three years ago, not fifty."

§

The next day, being Sunday, they had the whole day to themselves. "What would you like to do with our day off?" asked Nicholas.

"Let's explore the woodland running alongside the river."

"I'd love that. I spent a lot of time in those woods when I was your age. There are two stretches of woodland which are either side of the treeless area of the playing fields, etc. They are both good, but the northern stretch starting at the boathouse and reaching right down to the boundary of the school grounds, is the most beautiful because it is almost entirely beech trees."

They headed off to the boathouse and turned left to walk along a path beside the river. Looking ahead they could see a straight stretch of the river running along a valley whose flanks became steeper the further ahead they looked. The whole of the left side of the valley was clad in the glorious misty green of beech trees.

Nick turned off the path into the wood and walked on the soft, spongy surface produced by hundreds of years of fallen beech mast and leaf. He loved the look of the smooth algae-green bark of beech trees and reached out to stroke the tree he was passing.

"It's obvious that you love beech trees as much as I do. That's hardly surprising, of course. I'm sure we haven't changed anything that would make that kind of difference."

"Yes, we have a lot of beech trees in Sussex. Beech is my favourite kind of tree."

They continued through the wood with the ground they were walking on gradually getting steeper, sloping down from left to right.

"Nick, there is one more thing we should discuss in connection with keeping you off my anti-social habits. One of the most important things to think about when making and keeping friends is listening. Now you may think that listening is a very simple thing – just a matter of using your ears. But there is very much more to it than that."

"I suppose so; I've never really thought about it."

"Just so! Most people don't give it much thought. But it's actually very important to do so. The kind of listening I'm talking about is so much more than just hearing. A microphone can 'hear'. Human minds can do so much more. What I am talking about is often called 'active listening'.

"The first element of active listening is to be interested in what the person is saying. You may feel that sometimes people talk about very boring things. But it doesn't have to be boring. If you listen very carefully, thinking about all the implications of what they are saying, almost anything can become interesting. If you are not interested in what someone is telling you, it shows. What also shows very clearly is if, while you are listening, you are thinking of what *you* want to say next. Almost everyone does this at some time or another.

"Next, you must listen with understanding; if the person you are listening to says something which you do not understand fully, ask them to clarify it for you. They are unlikely to object to this as it is a good demonstration that you are interested in what they are saying. What people *don't* say can sometimes be even more important than what they *do* say. So if there seems to be a gap, ask about it. That is part of caring and being interested.

"It is also very important that you do not judge anyone. You may feel, for example, that somebody you are talking to has some bad attitudes about certain things. But those attitudes will only be there because something in their lives has caused them to be there. They can't help it; they didn't choose to have these attitudes, they were steered towards them."

"Are you sure about that?" said Nick. "Don't some people just choose to be nasty?"

"I believe from the bottom of my heart that they don't. I didn't always believe that. I learned to believe it as a result of the studying I did when I retired. There is a wonderful man called Nelson Mandela who is one of the leaders of the African National Congress which campaigns for equal rights for all people in South Africa. It was, I think, this year that he was imprisoned by the white government of the country. He will spend the next twenty-seven years in one of the worst and cruellest prisons in the world. During that time he will write his autobiography. Towards the end of the book, which he was presumably writing as he was nearing the end of his time in this inhuman prison, he was, nevertheless, able to write,

'There is at the heart of everyone a pure golden flame of goodness, which can sometimes become hidden, but can never be extinguished.' Those are probably not the exact words, but they are pretty close. I think they are a very good way to remind me that I have no business judging anyone.

"Finally, do your best to remember everything that your friend has told you. If the subject arises again in the future, and you cannot remember something that was said, it can be seen as evidence that you are not interested.

"If you can do all this for someone, or if they can do it for you, it is a huge step towards a good and lasting friendship."

They found that the slope which they were crossing was so steep that they could not continue ahead without hanging on to branches, shrubs and small trees. They decided to go carefully down the hill and back to the river. With much slithering, they reached the riverside path, which was now fairly narrow.

Looking into the river, the gentle movement of the current could be seen in ripples and flurries on the surface. Every now and then a fish would kiss the surface and ripple rings would radiate outwards. It was all so calm and silent that they sat beside the path and gazed at this world of peace, where all problems and worries disappeared, without exchanging another word.

A boy passed by in a canoe; he looked as if he was a third or fourth year. They called "Hello" to each other. This broke the spell and Nick said, "We'd better continue with our exploring." They got up and continued to walk along the path with the river to their right. "Thank you Nicholas for teaching me about active listening. I don't think I have ever thought about any part of it. But I will now. I've memorised a.....What's that word for a short set of words which reminds you of something more complicated?"

"A mnemonic?"

"That's the one. I've memorised 'Interest, understand, don't judge, remember' to remind me of the things I need to think of. That's my mnemonic." Nick grinned.

"Well done, Nick. You know that shows that you already have some listening skills. One part of active listening is the ability to summarise what you have been listening to. I didn't mention it because it isn't particularly relevant to the listening that goes on in day-to-day conversation. But it is certainly appropriate for you right now. Congratulations!"

"Thank you."

After a while they reached a brick wall ahead of them. They followed the path to the left and soon reached the school drive. Across the drive was an important looking stone gateway with statues on top of the gateposts.

"This is the boundary of the school grounds on the opposite side from the one you came through in the bus," said Nicholas. "Through the gateway is the village of Denfield. If you've brought your pocket money with you perhaps we could get something to drink at the village store. Would you like that?"

"Definitely. I have got my pocket money with me." Sunday was pocket money day and Nick had collected his five shillings this morning from Mr Bullen.

They decided to walk back along the drive. As they were walking, Nick said, "Nicholas, you always ask questions about what *I* would like to do. I have never heard you say what *you* would like to do. That doesn't seem right to me."

"Well actually I don't think that's true. In fact I can remember one occasion. When we went to my old house at Poynings, it was I who wanted to walk. But, for sure, I am very focussed on you. I'm not sure if you realise how important you are to me. You are my one chance to try and ensure that our life is not the awful misery that it was first time around. Why or how I have got this chance I have no idea. Nor do I know how long it will last. But I intend to do everything I can while it does last to see that you enjoy the great and fulfilled life that I never had."

"Nicholas, I know and understand that, and I'm not sure that you will ever quite know how grateful I am. But what on earth do you mean when you say you don't know how long it will last. How long will what last?"

"Nick, my dear boy, I mean I don't know how long I will stay with you – in your head."

Nick shouted out loud. "Nicholas, you're not to say that," he screamed. "Never, never, never say that again. I want you to stay with me for ever. You are the wonderful, beautiful father I never had."

# Chapter 10

A t 9:25 the following morning Nick was sitting in the waiting area of the medical centre waiting for his appointment with the doctor. The nurse came out and said that the doctor was ready for him. He went in.

"Good morning, Nick. My name is Doctor Dwyer. Nurse has passed on to me what you told her the other day, so I won't delve into that again. I know you found it distressing. I would just like to take a few measurements." He then did all the usual things that doctors do – pulse, blood pressure, temperature, peering into eyes and ears, stethoscope, the whole business. "I can't find any physical signs, but I didn't really expect to. With your parents' permission, I think we need to send you to a specialist."

"What sort of specialist, sir?"

"A psychiatrist."

"Do you think I'm mad, then?"

"I certainly don't. But it looks as if these blanking out episodes that you have been having are not coming from any physical cause in your body, but from somewhere in your head, and that's what psychiatrists specialise in. The man I am going to refer you to works in Lincoln. He is called Mr Henderson. He is very good. I have often referred patients to him before and he gets good results. Do you have any other questions you would like to ask me?"

"Do you have to tell my parents about it, sir?"

"The school has to obtain their permission, Nick."

"Well OK. They certainly won't mind, though, as long as it doesn't cost them much."

"It won't cost them anything. This is paid for by the Health Service."

Nick stood up. "Thank you for your help, sir."

§

*15ᵗʰ October 1963*
*Dear Mr & Mrs Harrison,*
*I regret to inform you that your son Nicholas is having some problems at school. He is experiencing occasional episodes where he appears to be in a coma, with his eyes open, but seeing and hearing nothing. I understand that this has also happened on two or three occasions at home.*

*He has been examined by the school doctor, who can find nothing physically wrong with him. He would like to refer Nicholas to Mr Henderson, a highly respected psychiatrist practising in Lincoln. I am writing to you to seek your permission for this referral to be made.*

*In all other respects Nicholas is doing well at the school. He has settled down well and his work is of a very high standard.*
*Yours Truly,*
*Anthony MacPherson, Headmaster.*

*17ᵗʰ October 1963*
*Dear Mr MacPherson,*
*Thank you for your letter. I'm sorry that Nicholas is being such a trial to you. I agree to his referral to Mr Henderson, and certainly hope that he can sort the boy out.*
*Yours truly,*
*Franklin Harrison.*

§

Nick was sitting in the tuck shop having a drink of lemonade when Tony Best joined him at the table. "Hi Nick,

I'm glad I've found you here. I've been wanting to apologise for being so rude to you at the swimming place the other day."

"You weren't rude, Tony. You were very upset."

"It was just that I was so ashamed at failing the swimming test, particularly after I had been boasting to you that I was a good swimmer."

"That wasn't boasting. You were swimming very strongly. It was just that you got into a muddle when you had to turn round. Most people find that tricky without a wall to push against."

"Anyway, you were very kind to me, and I wanted to thank you. Are we still friends?"

"Of course we are."

Nick wanted to punch the air and call out "Y-e-e-e-s."

"Well done Nick," said Nicholas briefly.

§

"I'VE GOT IT!"

"For God's sake Nicholas, don't shout like that. And anyway, not now; I'm in enough trouble already."

Nick was in his weekly French lesson. He turned his attention to Mr Flanders at the front of the class who was looking at him very strangely.

"Are you all right, Harrison?" Mr Flanders asked.

"Yes thank you sir. Perfectly."

When they got outside for their twenty minute break and there was no-one else around, Nick said, "What the hell was that about?"

"I suddenly realised that I do know of an important and dramatic event that is going to happen soon. I know the date and lots of detail. It's perfect for proving that our story is true."

"What is it? Tell me about it."

"What's the date today?"

"I think it's 20th October."

"Fantastic! The timing is just about OK, I think."

"Please tell me what it is that is going to happen."

"On November 22nd President Kennedy is going to be assassinated."

"Oh my God! How awful!"

"Yes, Nick, I know. Our first instinct should be to stop it happening. But think about it. How can we do anything to stop it? We're back to the fact that nobody would believe our story; not for one second. The assassination is unstoppable. The irony is that when it has happened, our story will have to be believed."

"So who should we tell our story to?"

"I think that Mr Henderson, the psychiatrist, will be the perfect person, because, I think I am right in saying that he cannot pass on anything about a patient, including what he tells him, without the patient's permission. We would need to check on that at the start of our session with Mr Henderson.

"The point is, it would still be our secret, between you, me and Mr Henderson. But when Mr Henderson discovers that our story must be true, he won't want to stuff us full of anti-psychotic drugs.

"I say that the timing is right because we can reasonably hope our first appointment with Mr H will be before November 22nd."

"How much detail about the assassination can you remember? The assassination itself ought to be enough, but any detail will make it even more convincing."

"I can remember quite a lot. In the early afternoon of November 22nd President Kennedy, his wife Jackie, the governor of Texas and his wife were travelling in an open-topped car as part of a motorcade. The streets were lined with well-wishers. Four shots were heard. Kennedy was shot through the head and died almost immediately. The Texas governor was shot in the back, but survived. In due course, one Lee Harvey Oswald was charged with the murder.

"He had taken up position in a room of a building beside the road called the Texas Book Depository – a warehouse for school textbooks – where he worked. The police subsequently discovered that only three of the four bullets they found had come from Oswald's gun, so there had to be more than one person involved."

"Wow! That *is* detailed."

"I doubt if there are many other events in my life which I could remember so clearly."

The outside bell had rung. Nick had a study period now, so he went to the library to work on one of his assignments. He found it very hard to concentrate.

That afternoon, after Nick had finished his rowing practice, Nicholas said, "I think it would be a good idea if I wrote down all of my Kennedy memories. Or rather, you would need to do the writing. I'm sure I wouldn't have the control to manage that. I can *walk* without your involvement, as we discovered on the downs. But I think writing would be far too complicated."

"OK, you'll need to give me some dictation. I guess that you want to do this so that you have something permanent to give to Mr Henderson, rather than relying on his memory of what you said."

"Just so. There is just one other possibility that I should point out to you. I am certain that none of the small changes we have made to the time-line could possibly have any effect on events in Dallas. But we have no way of knowing that what has happened to us never happens to anyone else. To give you an extreme example, if the elderly version of one of the senior White House staff has entered the mind of his younger self, it would be reasonably certain that the assassination will not happen. The White House man (or woman) would presumably be well able to arrange for the route of the motorcade to be changed. If something like that happens, then we will be in serious trouble."

§

When Nick got back to the school building, he checked in the 'H' pigeon hole and found there was a note for him. It said, *"Please will you come to see me in my room?"* It was signed by Mr Bullen. He had a shower, changed out of his games kit and went up to his housemaster's room.

"Come in, Nick. I have received a message that you have been given an appointment to see Mr Henderson in Lincoln at 10:00 on Tuesday 19th November."

"Oh, thank goodness for that!"

"I'm really glad you are looking forward to it. But please don't pin your hopes too high. He won't be able to make your problem go away in just one visit."

"Oh no, I understand that sir." (*"But two will do the trick,"* he thought).

"Mrs Platten has agreed to take you in to Lincoln, and bring you back afterwards. She has asked me to tell you to be at the medical centre at nine o'clock sharp. So please don't be late, Nick."

"I won't, sir. I promise."

# Chapter 11

M r Henderson's premises were in a beautiful Georgian building in the centre of Lincoln. Nicholas reckoned that he must be a very successful psychiatrist – the rent for offices in that building would be sky-high. Mrs Platten took them up to the right floor and rang the bell. The receptionist invited her to sit in the waiting room and showed a nervous Nick into Mr Henderson's office.

"Hello Nick, do sit down," he said, showing Nick to one of two comfortable armchairs. Mr Henderson sat in the other.

There was a silence until Nick said, "Before we start, can I ask if everything you hear from me is completely confidential, and won't be passed on to anyone, even my parents or anybody at the school?"

"Yes, Nick, that is correct. But there are two exceptions. I can pass on information in the unlikely event that I believe you to be a danger to yourself or to others. I also have to talk about my work at regular intervals to my supervisor, who is another psychiatrist. All therapists have to appoint a colleague to be their supervisor. I am, for example, a supervisor for two other colleagues. These rules are designed mainly for the protection of the clients. Does that all sound OK to you?"

"Yes thank you. It is what I had been hoping for."

"Good. Can you tell me why you have come to me for help?"

"In one way, no I can't because when….the thing happens, I am quite unaware of it. But other people, mostly some of the teachers at school, tell me that from time to time I go into what they call a sort of trance. Apparently, when this happens, my eyes are wide open – sort of staring, but it appears that I can see and hear nothing. To get me out of it, someone needs to shake me or poke me, or anything like that; I gather it's not difficult. But I can see that it must be very alarming for people who see it happening."

"You say that 'in one way' you cannot tell me why you're here. What about the other way?"

"That would mean telling you things that I have never told to anyone else. But that's fine. Because of the confidentiality I don't mind doing that for you. In fact it will be a huge, huge relief to tell someone. But I think it might be helpful if I demonstrate this 'trance'. This will show you that I am in control of it, and therefore know a little more about it than I have admitted up to now."

"Does it hurt you in any way to do this? Is it painful?"

"Not at all. In fact, as you will learn later, it is almost always a delight."

"Will you need me to shake you to get you out of it?"

"Well, you can if you want to. But I will make it last about thirty seconds or so if I can judge it correctly. Here goes!"

Nick had been sitting slightly forwards while he was talking. Now Mr Henderson saw him slump back into the chair and his eyes stared emptily ahead.

"Nicholas, how am I doing so far?"

"Brilliantly. I am most impressed. So far you are running the session in exactly the way you want it to go. But you do realise, don't you, that you can do that because Mr H is letting you."

"I hadn't thought about that, but I suppose you're right. But maybe that is how it normally works; maybe he knows that it can be the best way of learning what he needs to know."

"Maybe, although I'm sure that many of his clients won't play ball that way. After all, being referred to Mr H is exactly what we wanted, and it's all working out very well so far. Keep it up Nick; you're doing well. Now, I think your thirty seconds must be up."

Nick suddenly found that he could see his surroundings again. Mr Henderson was looking straight at him with a slightly puzzled expression on his face. "Welcome back, Nick! Are you all right? Do you need a drink of water?"

"No, I'm absolutely fine thanks. I do this a lot, although as soon as I learned what it looks like to other people, we've always tried to do it only when there isn't anyone else around."

"We? You said 'we'. Who's 'we'?"

"Woops! That's what I'm about to tell you. I'm sorry, the other half of 'we' told me I was trying to run this session. I hadn't realised it. I hope you don't mind."

"I certainly don't mind. It's what I always hope for from clients, but don't often get. So do please carry on. What's next?"

Nick grinned. "Well, now we get to the heart of it. This is the part that I have never told anyone, but desperately want to. But it's also hard because telling someone is a kind of point of no return." Nick paused and took a deep breath. "The main reason I have never told anyone about this is simple. Nobody could possibly believe it. It is completely ridiculous and breaks – no shatters – several scientific laws I imagine. There are two reasons why I feel I can tell you now. One is the confidentiality thing. The other is astonishing. We can provide you with solid proof that it is all real.

"So here goes: Several weeks ago, during the school holidays, I was awoken very suddenly and found myself jumping out of bed. A voice said, 'Oh God! Oh God! What the hell's going on?' I screamed and said something like, 'Who's that? Where are you?' I then realised that both things had come from my mouth. But it definitely wasn't me saying the first thing; it was someone using my voice somehow. To cut a long story short we eventually worked out between us that 'the other person' who had entered my mind was myself aged 63. We both still had our own minds and memories. When speaking to each other, I call him Nicholas, and he calls me Nick. Obviously Nicholas's memories include a rather thinned down version of mine, because, to him, they all happened a long time ago. At first we could only speak to each other by speaking out loud. This didn't involve any trance effect, but did involve me apparently talking to myself, which was almost as embarrassing as the trance. The amazing thing, to me, is how quickly we have got know and got used to each other. In fact, I now regard Nicholas as a very dear friend. We have spent a lot of time talking about the various issues which our situation raises, like the time-travel paradox and the importance of making any changes as small as possible, and so on.

"Now, I would like to hand over to Nicholas to tell you the rest of it from his point of view, if you wouldn't mind. His voice will sound exactly the same as mine, of course, because he is using my vocal chords. I know you don't, or rather can't believe a word of this, but please bear with us for a little while more, and then we'll let you get on with your job."

Mr Henderson smiled, "Worry you not. I'm doing my job by listening to you and to Nicholas. Never mind about what I believe and what I don't. I can assure you that I am riveted and fascinated by what you are telling me. So, your turn Nicholas"

"He didn't warn me he was going to do this, but, as ever with Nick, I think it is a very sensible idea. I think it will be helpful to you in one way or another for me to give you a sense of what all this is like for me and, perhaps, what it's about, from my point of view.

"Before all this started I was sixty-three years old, retired and living in a lovely cottage at Poynings in Sussex in the summer of 2013, in other words fifty years in the future. Without warning or presentiment, I found myself waking up one morning in a strange bed in a strange room. It was only strange, though, until I recognised the wallpaper as the one that was on my bedroom wall when I was a child. In utter horror I leapt out of bed and noticed that my body was that of a child. From then on it was as Nick described.

"I think it best, at this juncture, for me to tell a little about Nick's and my childhood up to the point where the impossible coming-together happened. We have had a truly horrible childhood. We are the second child of parents who only ever wanted one child. From the very earliest time our parents made this unwantedness very clear to us. We were given endless domestic chores to do; brother Jeremy was hardly ever made to do any. If there were no chores to be done we were required to make ourselves scarce and not come back to the house until evening. This started, so far as I remember, when we were about 6."

"That's right," agreed Nick.

"Mother and Father were always comparing us unfavourably with Jeremy, and they often said to us that they didn't love us at all, although we scarcely needed them to tell us this; they made it obvious in so many ways. Nick and I were sent away to boarding school from the age of seven, but not Jeremy. We assumed that they could not have done this because they wanted to give us a good education. So we realised that they hated us so much that it was worth the enormous fees just to be rid of us for four or five months of the year. In due course, from the moment I started my degree course at Loughborough College, I never again saw or spoke to my parents, and needless to say, they never wrote to me.

"Now I can imagine you feeling that I must be exaggerating the awfulness of this parenting. I promise I am not, am I Nick?"

"No way."

"The rest of my life has continued to be utterly miserable. This was for two main reasons – I hated myself, and I regarded everyone else that I ever met as stupid, boring or malicious. To my shame, it was not until I retired that I realised the reason for these feelings. When, in retirement, I had plenty of time on my hands, I decided that I would see if I could discover, through research into psychology books and papers, why I had always been so miserable and disliked everyone so much. Of course, Mr Henderson, you will know straight away what the answer to my quest was. I found that I had been taught by my parents how loathsome and unlovable I was, and it naturally followed that I thought everyone else must feel the same way about me. So the feelings of dislike that I felt for everyone else were, I now assumed, a kind of defence mechanism against their inevitable, as I believed it, dislike for me. I'm sorry! Digging that out has made me feel rather shaky. Does what I have told you about my assessment of the causes for my low self-esteem, and what resulted from that, hit the spot, do you think?"

"I'm not surprised you are feeling shaky; that was severely painful stuff you were exposing. It was very brave of you to do so. As regards your diagnosis, it sounds right. But I would not like to confirm it as a total explanation without having the opportunity to work with you. Is there anything else you want to tell me?"

"Oh yes! For me it is really the most interesting part, and one that I have not yet fully discussed with Nick. But actually I think he has been ready for it for some time. So here goes. The more I thought about this grotesque, impossible situation, the more I felt that there had to be a purpose behind it. And then I was struck by the coincidence of the fact that I had been sent to Nick when he was thirteen. And yes, I mean the word 'sent', for I believe that if there was a purpose, then I must have been sent by someone who understood that purpose. The coincidence is that I had none of my problems with myself or other people until I was thirteen and had started at Denport Abbey School. When I remembered this I knew that I had been sent back to try to save Nick from leading the same miserable life that I had led. I have really tried to do this, although I don't actually know what I am doing. But I guess what I have been trying to do is to teach Nick some relationship building skills. I think there are signs that it is starting to work. But he still needs so much more help from you. Nick has made some good friends at the school – something that I never achieved, even in the first term. So, together, we've made some small changes in the time-line, haven't we Nick?"

"We certainly have. I love it at Denport Abbey and it's great having all those new friends. But I know where you are going with this Nicholas, and I won't have it." Nick was sounding frightened and tearful, and Mr Henderson was looking concerned. "There is still such a lot to do, and I can't be doing it without you. I can't, I can't. Please don't leave me Nicholas. Please." Tears poured down his face and he howled.

When Nick had calmed down a bit, Nicholas very gently said to him, "Nick, do you think you could explain to Mr Henderson what's going on here?"

Between sobs, Nick explained, "Nicholas has already hinted that he might have to leave me, and now here he is saying it again. Why do you do this to me Nicholas?"

"Dear Nick, I was trying to explain to you yesterday that I think I may have no control over when I disappear."

"But why should you think such a stupid thing as that?"

"It is because I am certain, as I said, that I am here for the purpose of saving you from the destiny laid down by our parents. I don't want to leave you for as long as you need me or for as long as you think you need me. Mr Henderson and I will work on it together. I know I have helped you, and maybe I can help you some more. But, you know, the time will come when having me in your head will do more harm than good. How will you be able to become an independent, achieving individual with me in your head? What do you think about dating your first girl friend with me in your head? Now, we haven't reached the point of my doing more harm than good yet. But you know in your heart that point will come, don't you Nick?"

Nick nodded his head reluctantly and miserably.

"One more thing, Nick. I think you should tell Mr Henderson what you screamed out when I first let slip that I might have to leave you at some point."

Nick's voice was very small. "I said, 'Never say that again. I want you to stay with me for ever.'"

"And then you said?"

"You are the wonderful, beautiful father I never had."

Mr Henderson reached out and held Nick's hand. All was still for two or three minutes.

"Well now," said Mr Hendersen. "I think today has been an amazingly useful session. Thank you very much. But I think there's one thing you have forgotten. Your proof of existence, Nicholas."

"Ah, yes!" said Nicholas. "A few weeks ago I realised that there was just one way we could get anyone to believe what has happened to us. That would be if I could somehow remember some major headline-catching event which was about to happen. I thought very hard about this and realised there was one. We wrote it down to give you. I hope you've brought it with you, Nick."

"Of course I have," said Nick, and he pulled a slightly crumpled piece of paper from his pocket and gave it to Mr Henderson.

He read it through carefully. "My God," he said. "This isn't a joke is it?"

"In some ways I wish it was. He's a great man. But no, it is no joke. In three days' time, that is going to happen. It will be some time in the evening, British time, on 22nd November."

"I want to see you once a week, Nick. What day and time would suit you on a regular basis?"

"Monday afternoons would be best because that's my free afternoon every week, so I won't miss rowing or any classes. Is that possible?"

"That's a real stroke of luck. The Monday 2:00 slot has just become free. So I can see you every week at that time for the rest of the term. Then we can see if you need any more after that."

"Thank you very much," said Nick. He stood up and they shook hands.

Mrs Platten was waiting for them outside the front door. As they started the drive back to the school, she asked, "Well, how did it go?"

"Very interesting," said Nick.

# Chapter 12

On Friday, Nick and Nicholas knew that they had somehow to get hold of a radio to hear the 6:00 news. Then Nick remembered that his friend Charlie Bolton had said that he had one of the new transistor radios in his locker. So at lunch time Nick went over to where Charlie was.

"Hi Charlie, how are you doing?"

"Hi Nick. I'm fine. How are you? Have you been to see the specialist doctor person in Lincoln yet?"

"Yes, I went on Monday. He was a nice guy actually; I wasn't expecting that. Charlie, I wanted to ask you a big favour. I wondered if I could borrow your radio to listen to the six o'clock news on the Home Service this evening."

"Of course you can. I'll bring it to the junior common room at about quarter to. What's it all about?"

Nick had carefully prepared his lie. He hated to lie to a friend, but there really was no choice. "Oh, it's nothing really. Apparently my father may be interviewed on it, which will be a giggle."

"What's he done, then? Robbed a bank?"

"No, it's just something to do with his work, and they may not broadcast it at all. Apparently they only said they might use it."

Nick went to the common room at a quarter to six. Charlie and his tranny were already there. The radio was playing the Light Programme.

"Hi Charlie, can you tune it in to the Home Service please?"

Charlie retuned it. Nick didn't bother to listen to it as the news didn't come on till six. But he just wanted to make sure that everything was ready and nothing could go wrong. His heart was pounding. He couldn't help thinking of what Nicholas had said about somebody close to the president also receiving a time-traveller from the future. He supposed it didn't really matter that much, but he desperately wanted Mr Henderson to believe Nicholas.

Suddenly they heard words from the radio: "We are interrupting this programme to bring you a newsflash." Nick went weak at the knees and had to sit down. "We are receiving details of an assassination attempt on US President Kennedy in Dallas, Texas. At the moment this is all we know. We hope to be able to bring your more information in our six o'clock news."

Everybody in the common room was shocked to silence. Nick had to get outside somewhere where he could talk to Nicholas. Right now he did not know what to feel.

When they got outside with no-one around, Nick was almost in tears. "I just feel so guilty, Nicholas. It's as if *we* killed him."

"Well we didn't Nick. All that I did was to predict that it was going to happen. There was absolutely nothing that we could have done to save him. You know that, Nick, we discussed it."

"Yes, I know. But it doesn't stop me feeling the way I do."

It was only when he went into the dining hall for High Tea that Nick realised that he had completely forgotten about the six o'clock news. Charlie sat down opposite him. "Where on earth did you go? You missed the news."

"I know. Did they have any more information?

"Yes. The president was shot in the head. They didn't say he was dead, but it must be very unlikely that he could survive that. There were three other people in the car – Jackie

Kennedy and the Governor of Texas and his wife. The Governor was shot in the back, but it sounds as if he will survive. Oh, and there was no mention of your father."

"Oh, that doesn't matter."

So far Nicholas had got it all correct. No doubt they would hear in the next week or two about Lee Harvey Oswald and the building where he was waiting with his rifle.

After the meal, Nick went to the scrubland at the back of the gym so that he could talk to Nicholas unobserved. "It looks as if everything has worked out perfectly, Nicholas. You're a genius. I can't wait to see Mr Henderson again."

"Yes, that meeting will be interesting."

His voice sounded faint to Nick. "What's happened? Your voice is very faint."

"Is it? It didn't seem faint to me. But I'm not surprised. I am afraid it's beginning to happen, Nick. I'm so sorry."

Nick took a deep breath and bit his lip. "I'm not going to blub this time. I have accepted that you are going to leave me ever since you spoke about your 'purpose' to Mr Henderson. I just wish it didn't have to happen yet. Can you hang on until we go to Mr H on Monday?"

"I don't know Nick. I will if I can."

Nick had never felt more like crying without actually doing so.

§

When Nick arrived at reception at Mr Henderson's office, he rushed out to greet Nick. "Come on through, Nick. Do sit down." He seemed very agitated, his face looked grey and there were dark shadows under his eyes.

"Are you all right, sir? You look....I don't know....ill."

"No, I'm not ill, Nick. I'm in deep shock. Not so much because of the death of poor Kennedy, though, God knows, that was bad enough, but because the basis of what I have always regarded as reality has been turned upside down. I have hardly slept at all since Friday. Nicholas's prediction was so terribly accurate and detailed that, yes; I have to accept that your account of what has happened to the two of you is true."

Nicholas spoke aloud in a soft, quivering voice. "Thank you Mr Henderson for all you have done and will be doing for Nick."

"Are you all right?" answered Mr Henderson. "You don't sound so good."

"I am afraid it's happening. I feel.... as if I am fading away."

There was a short silence, interrupted only by one small sob from Nick. "I am afraid I don't really know what to say," said Mr Henderson. "That's rather unlike me. But all this is utterly beyond my experience and understanding. I promise you Nicholas that Nick and I will continue to work together for quite a while, if you agree, Nick."

"Of course, sir. I know that I….."

His eyes suddenly became glassy and sightless. A tiny voice in Nick's head said, "I'm going. I'm so sorry. Goodbye, Nick. Have a wonderful life." Nick's mind suddenly seemed to become flat.

"What's happened, Nick?" Mr Henderson asked.

"He's gone, sir. I know he wanted to stay longer. He couldn't help it. What am I going to do? I will miss him so much." Tears that had been forced back were now released. After what seemed like an hour to Nick but was actually about five minutes, he dried his eyes and took a deep breath. "I'm sorry, sir."

"That's perfectly OK, Nick. You needed that. Now, we still have another 50 minutes left of this session. But you may prefer to leave it for now and we can continue next week."

"Oh no! Please no sir. I badly want to talk now. Please! Please!"

"That's fine. I would like to start by asking you if you would call me by my first name, Alex. Is that OK?"

"Yes, sir….Alex, I mean."

"Can you tell me what you know about Nicholas, and what you felt about him?"

Nick thought for a while. "When he suddenly arrived in my head, I told you about that, didn't I, I was terrified of him. Even when he had tried to explain what had happened, I just wanted him to go away. I felt certain that I was going mad. I knew that hearing voices wasn't good. At first we could only talk to each other by speaking aloud. But that made it even worse; it seemed as if I was talking to myself, and that's not good either, is it?"

"You mean that you think talking to yourself is a sign of madness?"

"Yes."

"I can assure you that it isn't. Everybody talks to themselves from time to time. It's perfectly normal."

"Anyway, at first, as well as being scared out of my wits, I also didn't believe a word of what he was telling me. What he was saying was absurd and impossible. He was just a voice I was hearing." Nick shuddered at the memory of it. "But then, when I had calmed down a bit, I remembered that he had talked about a photo of himself, aged 13, that he had at home. I remembered that he had told me that mother had taken it, when he had asked her to, just after she had taken one of Jeremy. I realised that I had not said anything to Nicholas about mother having taken Jeremy's photo first. So it seemed that the only way he could have known about that was if his story was true.

"At first I hated him. He was a voice that had no business being in my head. I just wanted him to go away. This changed slightly after he had provided the photograph evidence. I had some respect for him, although I still wanted him gone, but I started to see him….I don't know….as a challenge for me to respond to, I suppose. But this rapidly changed during our first walk on the downs."

"Oh, you haven't mentioned walking on the downs to me before. It sounds interesting. Please tell me all about it, Nick."

"It seems incredible to me now, but it was on the same day that Nicholas arrived. Mother had kicked me out of the house for the day, which was great. Thinking about what we could do, I suddenly had an impulse to see Nicholas's house in Poynings. I still don't know why I wanted to do that then, but I suppose there was a small part of me that had already accepted Nicholas and the truth of his story. He suggested that we could walk there across the downs. I was horrified at first, thinking that it would be a real drag. I had never before done any real walking – you know, hiking. I reluctantly agreed.

"Alex, I can't tell you how wonderful that day was. I can vividly remember every second of it."

"I would like you to describe it to me in detail – what you did, what you saw, what you said to each other – all the things that made it so wonderful."

"I shall so enjoy doing that. I have obviously never talked with anyone about it, apart from Nicholas, and I never even talked with him about it, other than during the walk. So here goes:

"As soon as we had left Lewes behind us and were walking up the gentle slope of the downs, I knew that I was experiencing something very different....very special. The downs seemed to have their own smell – a lovely mixture of earth and grass and openness. There just aren't the words to describe it. There was a gentle wind blowing which was just strong enough to ruffle my hair a bit, and my legs felt strong and useful, surprisingly easily driving me up the hill. I felt so alive, with all the black things in my life left behind me. Oh, Alex, I'm sorry; am I just drivelling?

"You most certainly are not. This is exactly what I want to hear about, and you are telling it to me so vividly – from your heart more than from you head. I feel very privileged to be hearing it. Please carry on."

"When we got up to the ridge of the downs at Blackcap, there was a trig point. I had never seen one before and had no idea what it was. Nicholas explained it to me very clearly. I remember thinking that he would be a good teacher. The view from the top was astonishing. It was a very clear day and you could see huge distances. Nicholas pointed out all the things we could see. It suddenly struck me that he was a very interesting person to be with. We continued the walk following the South Downs Way along the ridge of the downs. I felt the most extraordinary feeling of belonging with my home county spread out below me. This was a feeling I had never even come close to before. My previous experience of Sussex was almost entirely confined to Lewes town. I had never felt that I belonged in the Harrison home – my feelings had always been more those of an unwelcome guest.

"So this whole walk was crammed with new feelings and new experiences to the point where I felt like a completely new 'me'. I couldn't help admitting that it was all down to Nicholas. What I felt about him was changing throughout the walk. Later, we experimented with trying to speak to each other in my skull – without having to speak aloud. We soon managed it. This was a great relief.

"We also talked a lot about the problems arising from time travel, or rather Nicholas did. Again, I was impressed by the way Nicholas explained things so clearly. I really learned so much from him on that one day. But Nicholas was also learning. It was during this walk that he learned how to *do* things as well as silent talking. We sat near the top of Ditchling Beacon to have our picnic lunch – I suppose it was Nicholas's as well as mine. When we had finished, I suddenly stood up as Nicholas was saying 'We had better make a move'. It wasn't me who stood up; Nicholas had learned how to do it for himself.

"When we reached Poynings, he stopped outside a gorgeous old thatched cottage. This was Nicholas's retirement home. I think we both desperately wanted to see inside, but knew we couldn't. It was somebody else's house then, of course. I could tell that Nicholas was feeling very wobbly about seeing it and feeling very weird wondering if he was looking at his past or his future.

"On the journey home I think we neither of us wanted to talk; we both had powerful things to think about. I reflected on the incredible, astonishing, beautiful and wonderful day I had had; the best of my life so far by a huge margin. I thought of the many things I had learned, of the spectacular viewpoints and what could be seen from them. Most of all I thought about walking on the downs, the richness of the experience, the delight of walking on the soft and springy downland turf, the feeling of achievement on reaching the top of a steep climb, the joy of sharing such a special world with rabbits and skylarks. And then I wondered about who it is that provides a thirteen-year-old boy with such treasures. I realised that this was what fathers do. Some fathers, anyway. This was the first time that I discovered that I felt about Nicholas as I would about a father. I so much wanted to hug him." Nick dropped his head and fell silent. He looked drained and exhausted.

"Thank you so much, Nick. I think you are an amazing boy. You have gathered together your memories and feelings about that extraordinary walk and expressed them so vividly. I know that you urgently wanted to do that, but I suspect it has not been as easy as perhaps you expected. Very well done! I think this is a good moment to finish for this week."

"Thank you Alex, I'm fine. Thank you so much for letting me do that."

# Chapter 13

Throughout the following week Nick was feeling close to despair. His classes and assignment work helped to distract him from his loss to some extent. He thought that the way he was feeling now must be the same as someone whose father had just died, assuming that he had been a proper father and not like his shrivelled up loveless creature. All that week he tried to avoid having to talk to anyone; he must save it for Alex. He knew that he was probably behaving in a way that would have worried Nicholas, but he couldn't help it.

At last, Monday afternoon arrived. Nick hurried into Alex's office.

"Hullo Nick. I have been thinking about you a lot this week. I imagine it has been a very tough week for you. How have you been coping?"

"Not very well at all. My school work has been a helpful distraction, but otherwise I have been trying to avoid people as much as possible. The trouble is that this is really the exact opposite of the way Nicholas would have wanted me to behave. Nicholas dies and I go completely off the rails, ignoring everything he taught me. That's an irony, isn't it?"

"It's completely understandable. If you *had* tried light-hearted chatter with your friends, it wouldn't have worked, would it? They would very soon have realised that something was wrong, and you wouldn't have been able to talk about how you were feeling without opening Pandora's Box."

"I know" said Nicholas miserably.

"I think what you need to do this afternoon is to talk a lot more about Nicholas, if you feel you can manage this without too much pain."

"It's the only thing I want to talk about, Alex."

"Did he tell you anything about his life?"

"Yes, quite a lot really." Nick paused to collect his thoughts. "Throughout his whole life he seems to have been miserably lonely. He told you himself why this was. My parents obviously made a very thorough job of teaching us how utterly worthless we are. Because of this, he never seemed to have been able to make any friends; he thoroughly disliked everyone, and I guess they probably disliked him. One of the effects of this was to cause him to move on frequently from one job to another and, later, from one country to another in an attempt to escape from unpleasant people and in the desperate hope of finding people who would even want to be friends with him.

"It wasn't until he retired and did his psychological research that he discovered the reason for all this – that our parents had taught us that we were worthless, unlovable people." Nick felt drained of all hope after recounting this dreadful story. "Alex, I'm so scared. How can I realistically avoid all this happening to me?"

"Because there are three of us – you, Nicholas and me – who are going to be working very hard to make sure it doesn't.

"But Nicholas can't any more. He's gone," Nick said miserably.

"Do you know, that's not true. Nicholas is still with you in your memories, and in all the things that he's taught you, isn't he?"

"Yes, I suppose so."

§

Nick was walking along the main corridor at school when a boy came up to him with a sneer on his face. "Aha! You're that fruit cake aren't you? Is the shrink managing to cure your madness?"

Nick didn't know the boy; he thought he was probably a third year. He was thinking about how to respond in a way which would be approved of by Nicholas. "No, I'm not mad, but I *am* going to see a psychiatrist every week. Why do you ask?"

The older boy looked surprised at Nick's admission. "Wouldn't you like to know?"

"Not particularly. I was just curious. My name's Nick Harrison. What's yours?"

"David Wenham." He gave his name automatically, and then wished he hadn't. "The whole school's talking about it, you know."

"Yes, I would imagine they are."

"Did you want it to be kept secret?"

"Yes, I suppose I did. It's a bit embarrassing when everyone knows about it, but it's nothing to be ashamed of. I guess you can't keep anything secret in a school. Is madness something that worries you?"

"No, not really. Look, I'm sorry I said that," David mumbled.

"That's OK, David. Not a problem. See you around."

"Yes, sure." David hurried away.

I hope that was OK, Nicholas. I wish you were still here to tell me, Nick thought.

§

"What I would like you to do for me now, Nick," said Alex "is to tell me about what Nicholas has taught you."

"Oh, he's taught me so much; some of it I don't think I can put into words – like how he has changed the way I think.

But I will do the best I can. First of all, he has helped me to understand how much I have been damaged by mother and father. He has also explained that almost everything he has been teaching me is aimed at trying to undo that damage.

"He has also taught me a great deal about making and maintaining friendships. On a number of occasions when someone has said something to me which was unfriendly, and I have been surprised by it, he took the opportunity, to talk it through with me afterwards. But instead of telling me what I should have done, he had a brilliant way of asking me a series of questions, like 'Why do you think he said that?' and 'What do you imagine he was feeling?' At first I found these questions hard; I often didn't think I knew any answers to questions like that. But every time Nicholas insisted I had a go at these questions, and it always seemed that I ended up understanding what had been going on in the boy's mind. It was amazing. Nicholas was such a good teacher.

"One of the really important things he helped me to understand is that people are driven to do and say things by what's inside them – by the sum total of everything they have experienced up to that time. I now know that there is no such thing as bad people, just damaged ones. Does this sound right to you, Alex?"

"Completely, Nick. I don't disagree with a word of it. But I think it is fair to say that there are plenty of people who would totally disagree, as you will undoubtedly discover, if you haven't already."

"That's great that you agree, although I didn't really expect you not to. The thing is I have found that Nicholas's way of saying 'What do I think is going on here?' when someone has said or done something nasty is incredibly good at helping to defuse the situation.

"Just last week a third year boy I didn't know came up to me and said, 'Aha! You're that fruit cake aren't you? Is the shrink managing to cure your madness?' It made me feel very angry. But I took a few seconds to think how Nicholas would like me to respond." Nick went on to tell Alex about the rest of the conversation. "The great thing was that it ended up with David apologising for what he had said, even though I wasn't able to work out what was going on inside his head. I thought it might have been because he was afraid of madness, but I don't think that was right."

"Well it could have been," said Alex. "Can you think of anything else it might have been?"

"Now you're doing a Nicholas," said Nick with a grin. "That's good." He stopped to think about what might have been going on with David. "Well, it doesn't answer the question, but I suppose what he was doing could be described as mild bullying."

"OK! And why do you think he was bullying you in this way?"

"Perhaps he bullies because it gives him a feeling of power over someone else and he likes that feeling."

"Perhaps."

Nick realised that Alex was waiting to see if he had anything more to say. He racked his brains. "Well, I suppose he may have been bullied himself in the past and so he now bullies other people – a kind of getting his own back. Perhaps that's why he feels compelled to do it."

"Both those explanations make a lot of sense, Nick. You're thinking well. Now you have explored these various possibilities, how do *you* feel about David's outburst?"

Nick explored his mind. "Well I certainly don't feel angry about it anymore. I also feel that going through this process of questioning what I think might be happening in David's skull is very useful.

"Anyway, Nicholas pointed out to me that the fact that there are no bad people, just damaged ones, makes it extremely important to take care that we never judge people. We should try to understand them instead. This feels absolutely right to me. But I find it extremely difficult; I often find myself judging people. It sort of creeps up on you. I think

I manage not to express judgement out loud to anyone. But I would love to be able to banish judgement altogether from my mind."

"If you were able to do that, Nick, I think you would be one of the first people in the world to achieve it."

"Another really important thing – well I think it is anyway – that Nicholas taught me is all about what he called Active Listening. Have you heard of that, Alex?"

Alex smiled. "Yes, I have. And I agree that it is a powerful way of getting to know someone, and enabling them to get to know you. But it needs lots of practice."

"Yes, it certainly does. I practice it a lot."

They sat in comfortable silence for a while.

§

Nick continued to visit Alex every week for the rest of that term. A lot of the time was spent telling Alex of various events, friendships and conflicts at school. By his last session, Nick was confident that he was well placed to beat off the dark legacy of his parents. He understood that they were simply responding to their own damage. He was also able to believe that he, Nick Harrison, was a fine human being with many great qualities. But he was also still afraid – afraid that it was all too good to be true. Alex said that he would still have wobbly moments from time to time, but that he had the strength and belief to overcome these.

"And don't forget, Nick, you can always come and see me again if you feel that it might help you through a bad patch. In any event, I would really like it if you can find the time occasionally to write to me to tell me about your life and the things that are happening in it. You are very special to me you know."

"Thank you Alex. And you and Nicholas are very special to me. Thank you for everything."

# Chapter 14

Nick was determined to justify all that Nicholas and Alex had done for him. He worked hard on his social life, carefully putting into practice all he had learned from them. To his delight and profound relief he found that this all became easier until, after a couple more terms at school, he no longer had to work on it – it just seemed the natural way to be. He found that he had formed many friendships at the school.

He also wanted to do as well as possible with his school work so as to get the best possible grades in his O and A level exams. Keeping the right balance between the social and academic sides of his life was, he found, harder than he had expected. There were often times when friends would ask him to join them in free time activities when he knew that he had to put the time into his assignments or doing some background reading. Almost always he opted for studying.

He limited himself to model-building in the Model Railway Club for just one evening per week although it was something he loved doing. He joined the school drama group with some hesitation, as he had never done anything like that before. He discovered that acting was a deeply rewarding activity, although he worried about the amount of time taken up with learning his lines.

On reaching the third year he took part in the course to train to become a swimming life saver. It was a tough course which some of the participants did not pass. So Nick was delighted when he passed and went on to discover the pleasure and satisfaction of saving swimmers in trouble. It was also in this term that he took the Cambridge University entrance exam with the aim of gaining a scholarship to Trinity College. This he obtained provided he got two A's and a B at A level.

Every term he wrote to Alex to keep him posted of his life and times. To his great delight Alex always replied. In one of these replies he mentioned that he was due to retire in 1967. Nick was amazed; he could scarcely believe that Alex was that old.

§

"Come in, Nick. Have a seat," said Mr Lamont, Nick's tutor. "As you probably know, now that you are nearing the end of your third year it is my job to talk you through your options for what subjects you would like to study during your last two years leading up to A levels. The first thing I need to ask you is if you have any ideas about what sort of career you want to follow when you have finished school and university. Bear in mind that you do not have to make these kinds of decision at this stage. But if you do know what you want to do, it should help you to decide on your A level subjects."

"I've been thinking about this quite a lot. I know what I want to study at university – quantum physics."

"Good heavens, what brought that on?" said Mr Lamont with a smile.

Nick looked uncomfortable. "Well, I don't know really. I have been reading up about it and it sounds a really interesting subject. I suppose that's partly because it's right on the frontiers of physics."

"That sounds like a good reason for someone like you to want to do it. I'm sure you don't need me to tell you that you are a quite exceptionally able boy."

"Thank you, sir!"

"We fully expect you to get excellent results in the eight subjects you sat at O level."

"So, I suppose I will need to take physics, pure maths and applied maths at A level, won't I?"

"Yes, that's what you will need to get a place on a natural sciences course at Cambridge."

"And I would also like to do biology at A level."

"In your case that will be fine. I'm sure we can work out a timetable for you to follow those four courses."

§

*15ᵗʰ June, 1965*

*Dear Alex,*

*I am hoping you may be able to help me with a bit of advice about something. I've just had a session with my tutor to decide on what subjects I want to take at A level. It was all a bit difficult really. I have known for some time now that I want a career researching into time travel. Of course, you and I are the only two people in the world who understand why I must do this. I obviously can't talk about this to my tutor, or indeed anyone else apart from you. So when my tutor asked what I wanted to study at university, I said quantum physics. And then, of course, he wanted to know why. I said something a bit lame like it sounded like an interesting subject. Anyway, he let it go at that and he agreed that I should do A level physics, pure maths, applied maths and biology. I added the biology because I would love to know what was going on when Nicholas was in my head.*

*Anyway, the point is that I am assuming that quantum physics is the best thing to do if I want to get a hold on time travel. Am I right? I realise that there's no reason why you should know. But I bet you know the sort of people you could ask questions like, 'I know someone who wants to do research into time travel. Would quantum physics be the best way for him to get there?'*

*I know I am asking a lot. But I'm stuck. You are the only person it is possible for me to ask about this.*

*I hope you are well. I was amazed when you wrote that you would be retiring soon. I didn't think you were anything like old enough.*

*With love from,*
*Nick.*

*30th June 1965*
*Dear Nick,*
*Thanks for your letter. I'm glad you asked me to help. It just so happens that I do know a couple of people who are the perfect ones to ask your question. They both agreed that quantum physics was exactly the right choice. They were quite amused by the question and were obviously dying to know who it was for. But they knew better than to ask me that!*

*I was most flattered that you thought I was too young to be retiring yet. I assure you I'm not. And unlike many people, I am really looking forward to retirement. I will let you know my new address in due course; at present I haven't even decided where I would like to live.*

*Do please let me know when you have received your O level results.*

*With love,*
*Alex.*

He had taken eight subjects at O level and achieved top grades in everything except English Literature, for which he obtained a B. He regarded this English Literature result as a shameful failure, although his friends all said that he should be ridiculously proud of his overall results.

§

In his fourth year Alex wrote to Nick to tell him that he had sold his business and retired. He had bought a house in Chesterton on the northern edge of Cambridge. He said that he thought it was great that Nick would be coming to

Cambridge University to do his degree; they might be able to meet up from time to time

§

In his final term at Denport Abbey, Nick pushed himself very hard in the run-up to A levels. Quite a few of his friends and some of the teachers were becoming anxious about him. Nick simply explained to them that it was of massive importance for him to get the best possible grades in all his A levels if he was to do what he felt he must do at university and beyond; there was simply no question about it so far as he was concerned.

§

So it was that he was extremely agitated as he waited for the postman to deliver his results at home in Lewes. Nick grabbed the envelope and stared at it fiercely as if to force the contents to show the right results. With shaking hands he opened the envelope and snatched out the papers. It looked as if…..yes!…..he had got top grades in all four subjects. He fell in to a chair. He was shaking all over.

"Well, what have you got then?" his mother asked.

Nick passed the result sheet to her. "That looks all right, doesn't it?"

"Yes mother, that looks all right," he said in withering tones.

"Well, I don't know what you expect me to say"

"'Well done Nick!' wouldn't come amiss. 'You've done very well; you must have worked hard' would be perfectly acceptable. If you wanted to you could even say, 'You're a very clever lad; I'm proud of you'".

"You're getting too big for your boots. The only thing that matters is whether you are going to get a scholarship so that we don't have to shell out any more money for your education."

"Oh, I have already had the promise of a scholarship from Trinity College."

"What! Why didn't you tell me?"

"I didn't think you were interested as I knew that there was no question of you being willing to pay for it. I shall be out walking for the rest of the day."

§

Within a few days of starting at Cambridge, Nick knew that he was in his element and loved every second of it.

One evening he went with a small group of friends to *The Eagle* in Ben'et Street – a pub favoured by students. He knew that it was here that Crick and Watson first announced that they had 'discovered the secret of life' unravelling the structure of DNA. That made it an inspiring place, Nick thought. He and his friends were comparing notes on the various student societies they had joined. Nick had so far confined himself to the Trinity rowing club, worrying that if he got too involved with sport and recreation he would be risking taking his eye off the only thing that really mattered – getting a first. They also got to talking about their girlfriends, and the others were highly amused to hear that Nick didn't have one. "I haven't got time for that sort of thing," he protested unconvincingly.

"That's ridiculous. How do you think we manage?"

"Well, I suppose it's also that I'm shy about girls. I suspect I haven't had your great experience."

The others immediately decided that they were going to sort him out a girlfriend. Peter Drake, discreetly indicated a pretty girl sitting on her own on the other side of the room. "What about her?" he said. "She looks as if she's a student."

"Yes she is," said Nick. "I recognise her; she's doing the same course as me."

"What the hell are you waiting for then? Go and introduce yourself."

"I can't do that. I can't just walk up to her and say, 'Hi! I'm Nick. Who are you?'"

"Of course you can, you silly bugger. Although you can probably manage to say a bit *more* than that."

"But she's certain to have a boyfriend already – a girl as pretty as that."

"So what? Now she'll have two boyfriends. That's how it works."

"But supposing she….."

"Nick, shut up and just do it. We'll stay out of your way."

He had butterflies in his tummy. She really was a gorgeous girl. He got up and walked over to her. There was cheering in the background.

"Hallo! Do you mind if I join you? Do say if you'd prefer me not to."

She laughed, "I'd like you to. And well done for braving it; I thought they'd never persuade you."

"Oh my God! Could you hear what we were saying?"

"Every word. It was very entertaining." Nick felt desperately embarrassed. He started to get up. "No, please don't go. I wasn't meaning to make fun of you. It was very rude of me. I apologise. My name is Kristin Bruchner."

"I'm Nick Harrison. It's lovely to meet you. But it's just occurred to me, were you meeting someone else here?"

There was a pause. "Yes I was. But the bastard has stood me up."

"Oh! I'm sorry." He didn't know what he should say.

"Are you?" Kristin said with a smile.

"Well no, I'm glad actually. Is that wrong?"

"Not even slightly. Let me guess. Your school career was entirely in boys-only boarding schools, and you hardly know what girls are; they're an alien species. Am I right?"

"Yes, I'm afraid you are." He wanted to change the subject "Which college are you in?"

"Trinity."

"So am I."

"Yes I know. I've seen you about." Nick felt that he was permanently on the back foot. Kristin must think he was a naïve little boy. Oh God, he was completely out of his depth. Kristin took hold of his hand. "Nick, don't look so worried. You're doing fine. I think we should get to know each other. Is that OK with you?"

"Yes, it's certainly OK with me, although I don't know why you'd want to bother."

"Why do you run yourself down like that?"

"Ah, now that's a long story. I'll tell it to you sometime."

§

They had arranged to meet again on the following Saturday afternoon on Magdalene Bridge over the Cam by the punting station. As Nick walked down Bridge Street he could see that Kristin was already there. He saw her beautiful, shining fair hair dancing lightly in the breeze, and his heart lurched; she was such a beautiful girl. He ran to her. "Sorry, am I late?"

"No, I was early."

It was a beautiful, warm autumn day and they strolled along The Backs beside the River Cam with its glorious assortment of swans, ducks and punts.

"I'd love it if you will tell me all about yourself – the things you've done in your life, the things you love and the things you hate," said Nick.

"OK! I was born and brought up in Germany. I have an older brother and a younger sister. My dad is a solicitor, my mum is a teacher; she teaches English at a Gymnasium. That's a type of school that is more or less the equivalent of the

British grammar school. I was educated at the same Gymnasium where my mother was a teacher. This was *not* a great arrangement as it meant that I had to behave better than any of the other kids."

"How do you come to speak perfect English?"

"Oh, it's not perfect; I definitely have a German accent. But it's pretty good, I suppose. It's partly because, once I had been learning English at school for a year or so, my mother would always talk to me in English and insisted that I did the same to her. But also, when I was 16, I transferred to an international school here in England. It had a full-range curriculum, but everyone had to speak English at all times. About half of the kids were English, and the rest were from countries all over the world. Everyone boarded at the school – even the English kids. The school was near Kendal in the Lake District, and things like orienteering and rock climbing were organised for us as well as normal classes. I met all sorts of amazing people there. I'm still in touch with some of them. And now I've started at Cambridge – and met you, which is definitely another plus. What do I love and what do I hate? Well, I love England and the English. And I love Cambridge. I love Germany. I love people. I don't think there's anything I hate really, except, perhaps, people who allow their dogs to shit on the pavement."

"What are your parents like? Do you get on with them?"

"Oh yes definitely. They are both beautiful people and I love them dearly. I've had a very good life, up to now. But now it's your turn, Nick. What sort of life are you having?"

Nick felt unsure quite how to respond. He didn't want to introduce what might seem like a sour note. But he didn't want to be telling Kristin any lies. He decided not to pull any punches about his parents and Jeremy, and he did tell her about going to see Alex for a term. But he knew he couldn't tell her about Nicholas, for the usual reason – she wouldn't be able to believe it. He explained that Alex had been helping him with his social skills. He was great, and they had remained friends ever since. He also told her about the joys of walking on the South Downs.

"Oh Nick, how awful for you. I can't imagine what it must be like to hate your parents and for them to hate you."

Nick noticed with alarm that there were tears in Kristin's eyes.

"Please don't worry about that. Of course it's rather sad in a way. But I have learned to blank that out and just get on with life. And I have now, at last, got rid of them. I won't be seeing them or speaking to them ever again. I will find somewhere to live in Cambridge, and get temporary jobs to keep me going during the vacations."

Kristin gave him a long hug, which turned seamlessly into a kiss.

# Chapter 15

"Hi Alex! It's Nick."

"Nick! How wonderful to hear you. How are you? Are you settling into college all right? Are you enjoying the course?" Alex asked.

"What a lot of questions all at once. I was wondering if I can come and visit you some time. If so, I could answer all your questions then."

"I would love that. When can you come?"

"I'm free tomorrow afternoon. Would that be OK?"

"Perfect. Would you like me to come and pick you up?"

"No need, thanks. I've bought a second-hand bike. I discovered that you can't be a Cambridge student without owning a bike. I'll see you tomorrow at about two o'clock."

§

Kristin was talking to her friend, Barley Green in the Trinity combination room. Barley had been a student at the same international school that Kristin had been to and they had become close friends.

"Barley, you know that boy, Nick Harrison, whom I met last week at *The Eagle*?"

"Yes, you told me you fancied him? What's new? Tell me! Tell me!"

"Well we met up again today. Well….This is just between you and me, OK?"

"Yes, of course."

"He's quite unlike any other guy I've ever met. It turns out that he seems to have had a pretty tough life."

"Oh dear! Please tell me he's not another of your lame ducks."

"No he's not. He's had a tough life, but he's no lame duck. I get the feeling he is very strong-willed. He seems to be pulling himself out of the mire by sheer determination. His mum and dad sound like the parents from hell. All his life they've repeatedly made it clear to him that he is the unwanted second child, and they don't love him at all. He told me today that he is never going back home again – he's going to stay in Cambridge during the vacs. He seems to find a great relief in knowing that he will never again see or speak to either of them.

"God, how heavy is that?"

"Yes, but underneath all that there is great power and determination. There is also a feeling of mystery about him. There's something he's holding back, I think. I just want to be with him all the time, Barley."

"That's great, Kristin. But please take care. You may have got hold of a time bomb."

"Look, I'm sorry; I've got to dash. I've got a tutorial in ten minutes."

Kristin had a lot of respect for Barley. Could she be right about Nick being a lame duck and a time bomb? Kristin wondered. She couldn't see it somehow. Lame ducks wouldn't have the focus, drive and determination that Nick has. These are all admirable qualities, of course, but they wouldn't always fit too well with personal relationships – and love. Kristin knew she was in love with Nick. A couple of times in the past she thought she had been in love, but this was something else; very different from anything she had known before. Perhaps this was interfering with her ability to make rational decisions. And what about Barley's time bomb? There must be a limit to how hard Nick can push himself. What would happen if he passed that limit? It scared her just to think of it. Damn it! Stop worrying, she thought. Just let it all happen – for now, anyway.

§

"Hi Nick! How did you get on with that girl in the pub?" It was Peter Drake.

"OK, I think."

"OK you think? Is that all you have to say to the genius who pushed you in the right direction? What's her name? Have you been with her again?"

"Well, I must admit it was the right direction....I think. I mean I don't know anything about these things. When I'm with her I don't know if I am saying the right thing or doing the right thing. But I feel like I've been bewitched. I can't stop thinking about her. Oh Peter, she is so beautiful, and she is also very lovely person – very intuitive and sensitive."

"Oh my God, you have got it bad. What did you do when you went out with her again?"

"We walked along The Backs, and we talked and talked – exchanging life stories mostly. And then, at the end, she kissed me."

"Oh man, you're home and dry."

"I'm not at all sure about that. I mean I know I'm completely overwhelmed by her in a way I have never experienced in my life before. But I'm sure she must think I'm very boring....and rather weird as well, probably."

"What? Why on earth would you think that? Keep calm, man. Just relax and stop making assumptions about what she might think."

§

The next day found Nick arriving at Alex's address in Chesterton. It was a rather grand Victorian house with wooden balconies under both the first floor windows and wisteria-covered walls. Nick thought it looked rather large for two people, but perhaps they had a lot of furniture of sentimental value that they couldn't bear to part with. Nick rang the bell. When Alex came to the door they gave each other a big hug. "Come on through," Alex said and led Nick through to a large veranda which stretched the full length of the back of the house. It overlooked a large, immaculate garden.

"What a beautiful garden!" Nick said.

"Yes, isn't it. I can claim no credit for it. It's all Jenny's work; she is a passionately keen gardener."

"Is somebody taking my name in vain?" said a smart and slightly forbidding-looking woman as she bustled on to the veranda.

"Ah, meet my wife, Jenny. Jenny, my dear, this is Nick Harrison."

"It's lovely to meet you at last. I know you two have been exchanging letters for years now."

"How do you do?" said Nick. "It's lovely to meet you too."

"Now, Nick, you will stay for tea later on, won't you."

"That's very kind of you. I'd love to. Thank you Mrs Henderson."

"No! No! Please call me Jenny. 'Mrs Henderson' makes me sound like an appendage to this old chap."

Nick wasn't sure what to make of this. It sounded almost rude. But he supposed it was simply humorous, and he had to admit that he would hate to be called Mr Harrison by anyone.

"Now, if you'll forgive me, I'll leave you two to do some catching up. My garden is calling me for my attentions."

"Sit down, Nick, and tell me all the things that have been happening in what must be very exciting times for you."

"Where to begin? I did tell you, didn't I, in one of my letters, that I had been lucky enough to get a scholarship to Trinity College. That was ages ago."

"Yes, you did, although I am absolutely certain that luck had nothing to do with it."

"I managed to get very good grades in all four of my A levels. So here I am, a student at Cambridge University. I still can't really get my head round that. I suppose I will eventually, although I hope I never get to take it for granted."

"That sounds as if you are enjoying it."

"Oh, Alex, I just love it. There are so many things I love about it. I'm really enjoying the natural sciences course, and it's really stretching me which is great. Trinity is a wonderful college, and I love my beautiful old room there. I am making lots of friends. I love the city of Cambridge; it makes me feel almost a part of history. Walking along The Backs seems almost too lovely for words. I am being treated like an adult human being for the first time. And, best of all, I have got rid of my parents. I will never see them again. You've no idea how free, independent and joyful that makes me feel. Although, come to think of it, you, of all people, probably do know that. Sorry, Alex, I'm just blathering on."

"You certainly aren't. But I wonder if *you* have any idea how wonderful it is to hear you so full of excitement with life, and so positive about everything. That is such a relief and a joy to me, even though I never really doubted it would happen."

"I'm so glad you feel that as so much of my present frame of mind is thanks to you."

"And to Nicholas. But you know, Nick, it *is* mostly your doing. I have always marvelled at the fierceness of your determination not to have to live the same life as Nicholas did."

"I'm so glad, Alex, that you still believe in Nicholas. I mean, that you still believe that he was a separate mind within my head who had travelled back in time from 2013."

"Of course I do Nick, and always will. How could I not. You and Nicholas provided the most watertight proof it would be possible to have."

"Yes we did, didn't we? Nevertheless, it doesn't alter the fact that if we hadn't had your trust and belief in us, I wouldn't be living the wonderful life today that I am"

"Nick, you said just now that you wouldn't be going back to your Lewes home ever again."

"I certainly won't. Anyway it isn't my home. It never was."

"What are you going to do in the vacations? You won't be allowed to stay on in the college, you know."

"I know that. I will get some digs somewhere in Cambridge and get a temporary job. I'll get it all organised nearer the end of term."

"I see." Alex looked very doubtful. "Tell me about your social life."

"Oh, it's great. I've made so many wonderful friends, and we have a really good time together. We go out to the pubs some evenings. They're more fun than the college bar. Actually I don't drink that much; I don't like what it does to you if you have more than a couple of pints. It's like losing control of yourself, and I can't bear to do that. I mean, I don't mind if others do it; that's up to them. But it's not for me.

"But the most amazing thing that's happened is that I have met a wonderful girl called Kristin. We've only been out together twice, but already I feel that I've known her for months. I never imagined that could possibly happen to me."

"Why not, Nick?"

"Oh all sorts of reasons. For one thing I didn't think any girl could possibly like me; they'd probably find me very boring. And anyway they would all have boyfriends already. And I don't know anything about girls; I don't really know what to say to them, or what sorts of things they like doing, and so on...." Nick tailed off, feeling rather embarrassed.

"So do you think Kristin thinks you're boring and dislikes you?"

Nick thought about this for a moment. "No, amazingly she does seem to like me and we get on very well together."

"How amazing is that?" teased Alex.

"I know it's silly really. But think about it – I've hardly ever met any girls before this last couple of weeks. I've no idea about what to expect. Anyway, on our second date we exchanged potted histories, and when it was my turn I had a bit of a problem. I felt I couldn't tell her anything about the Nicholas episode; she would probably just think I was fantasising and think I was just pathetic. I did mention *you* to her; I just said that you had been helping me with some social problems. But the thing is, I do want to tell her all about Nicholas, but in a context where she won't think it is fantasy. So I expect you can guess what I am going to ask you."

"Yes, the same as I was going to ask *you*. We would really love to meet Kristin."

"I'm so glad. But I would like to leave it for a few weeks. We hardly know each other at the moment, even though it doesn't feel like it. Who knows? In a few weeks we may have split up, although I cannot imagine how that could be. But I don't know anything about these things. In that case I will probably be coming on my own for tea and sympathy. But, if all goes well the idea would be, as I see it, for you and I to tell her the Nicholas story together, with you providing the evidence, as it were. Is that OK with you?"

"Yes, of course, I think that's a good plan."

"Does Jenny know about me?"

"Only that you are an ex-patient of mine and that we have been keeping in touch with each other by post."

"Well I would be very happy for her to join us in the big revelation, if you think she might be interested."

"That's fine. I will invite her to join us whenever it happens."

# Chapter 16

Several weeks later Barley and Kristen were strolling down Trinity Street to get a coffee from The Whin on the corner of Green Street and have a chat. Barley thought Kristin looked worried about something and she hoped that she would feel able to talk about it.

"What's wrong Kristin?" Barley asked after they had got their coffee.

"Not much gets past you. I don't really know what's wrong; it may be something very small. Nick is still the same gorgeous, sensitive, caring guy that I love so much, but for a few weeks now I have realised there was something worrying him. At times he has become quite agitated. Then yesterday he suddenly admitted that there was something about him which he had not told me. I told him that I had thought this might be the case. He then asked me to trust him a little longer, and then all would be revealed. He wanted me to come with him and meet an old friend called Alex who lives in Cambridge. He said that he and Alex would between them be able to explain everything. He knew, he said, that this must seem very weird and mysterious, but that she would completely understand everything after the visit. He said that Alex and his wife Jenny had invited them to their house for the day next Sunday, could I make that, and was I prepared to come?"

"Oh, my God! How did that make you feel?"

"My immediate feeling was that something had kicked me in the stomach. I felt angry that he had talked about us to someone I had never met. But then I realised that was a ridiculous thing to think. Completely phoney. After all, I have been happily talking to you about him right from the start, and he's never met you. Then I started wondering what the secret could be. Perhaps he wanted to tell me that he was queer, and that Alex was his boyfriend. But that was just absurd. I know bloody well he's not queer. He's proved it to me....very well, I might add.

"Then I remembered that when he was telling me his life story during that magical walk along The Backs, he mentioned that a psychiatrist he had visited for a while when he was thirteen was called Alex. Well, then of course I thought that they were going to tell me that Nick is mentally ill. But wouldn't I have noticed something odd about him after the last beautiful weeks. I really couldn't believe that. I also wondered if they were going to tell me that he had some ghastly terminal illness and had six weeks to live. But he wouldn't need a psychiatrist to help tell me about that. I didn't know what to think. I was in such a muddle. I still am. I just feel anxious and miserable. I feel I may be about to lose him."

Barley moved to sit next to Kristin on her bench seat. She put her arm round Kristin's shoulders. "Oh you poor thing. I can only imagine a fraction of what that must be like. Did you say you would go with him to Alex's house next Sunday?"

"Of course I did. I'm not letting my sweetheart go that easily. But I just want it to be Sunday."

§

On Saturday evening, Nick was sitting in the college bar. He was due to meet Kristin there in ten minutes. But he wanted a little time to collect his thoughts. He now knew for certain that he wanted to spend the rest of his life with Kristin, and he hoped – no strongly suspected – that she wanted the same. For him there was absolutely no possibility of there being anyone else. And here he was, possibly on the eve of losing her for ever. But surely that wouldn't happen. It was really no big deal at all. But she must think it so weird that he needed Alex to help him explain it to her. But that was only because she couldn't possibly believe it otherwise. He must explain that to her tonight.

"Hallo darling!" Nick jumped — he hadn't spotted her arriving. "Wow! You're jumpy." She kissed him tenderly.

"I'm sorry, sweetheart. I was lost in thought about the things I must tell you this evening. I'll just get us drinks from the bar."

When he returned, he said, "I think you must have been going through hell since I asked you about tomorrow's visit. I explained so inadequately. I can't imagine what ideas you must have been having since then."

"I'm really glad you can't. They haven't been good. But I'm still with you in spite of that because I love you, my darling one."

"And I love you. I could say so much more, but I think I should wait till after tomorrow to make sure I haven't lost you. Oh Lord, that sounds very ominous. Let me tell you straight away that I truly can't see why what you learn tomorrow will make any change in the way you feel about me.

"One of the things I should have explained when I suggested tomorrow's arrangements is that the reason I couldn't just tell you what this was all about is because what happened to me is completely impossible and you would be quite unable to believe it. The reason I need Alex's help is that he is the one that can prove that what we say is true."

Kristin was, for a moment, struck dumb. Then "Shit! I can't wait for tomorrow to come."

§

They cycled to the Henderson's house, arriving, as arranged, at 9:30. Jenny answered the door and Alex introduced Kristin. Jenny gave her a huge bear-hug and said,

"It's so lovely to meet you. Alex and I are very fond of this man of yours."

The sky was overcast but it was warm enough to sit on the veranda again. Jenny sat them down beside a table holding a huge jug of lemonade and four glasses. Alex joined them and was introduced to Kristin.

"Nick tells me you are from Germany."

"Yes, that's right, though I have spent more time in England than in Germany for the last two and a half years."

Impatient to get going, Nick took Kristin's hand and said, "You are going to hear a story today, darling, and one that is going to stretch your mind to its limits. But I promise you that every word of it is the truth." Through her hand he could feel that the poor girl was shaking. 'Let's get on with it! Let's get on with it!' his mind shrieked.

"When I was thirteen I woke up one morning at home......" He went on to tell her about finding Nicholas in his head and discovering that his mind was really there, as well as his own. He described the utter horror that they both felt, and how they quickly had to accept the situation, as there was no other choice. He told her how, at first, they had to speak aloud to talk to each other. He described the embarrassment that this caused, and his parents' negative and uncaring response. He then went on to tell her about Nicholas introducing him to the delights of downland walking, and how, on one of these walks, they learned to converse soundlessly. He told her about the side-effects of this method of talking, leading to Nick being referred to Alex. He also told her of Nicholas's account of his appalling, friendless, lonely and miserable life. He described Nicholas's desperate attempts to stop Nick from leading the same life. He explained how they were both desperate to be able to tell someone what was happening, and how they realised that they couldn't as they would not be believed. He described Nicholas's President Kennedy brainwave, and writing it down for Alex.

"That is everything that happened before I started to go and see Alex. So Alex, can you pick up the thread now please?"

He saw that Kristin's eyes were stretched wide with disbelief and horror, and could feel that she was still shaking.

Alex continued with his experience of Nick as a patient. "When Nick first came to see me, he took the session over from the word go – something I always used to appreciate from a patient, though it rarely happens. He told me everything he has just told you, and then, rather unusually, he handed it over to Nicholas to continue from the point when he realised the importance of being able to remember in detail the assassination of President Kennedy. They handed to me a written copy of Nicholas's prediction.

"Nicholas also talked about the parent-damage he had suffered, the resulting bad self-image and his total inability to make friends and other relationship problems. He said he hadn't the faintest idea how he had got into Nick's head but spoke of his increasing certainty that he should take advantage of the opportunity to try and help Nick to avoid the legacy of his parents and the awful life that he had experienced. This was done mostly by teaching Nick some social skills.

"When Nick left at the end of that first session, I was fairly stunned, I can tell you. Never in the whole of my career as a psychiatrist, before or since, have I come across anything remotely like this. Of course, I didn't, for one second, believe that sixty-three-year-old Nicholas was in Nick's head, nor did I believe that any time travel had taken place. That was, quite simply, impossible. Nevertheless, on November 22nd I found myself, slightly guiltily, listening in to the radio for any announcement. Then the announcement came and over the next few days I discovered that Nicholas had been correct, including all the many details he had provided.

"President Kennedy's assassination was a great shock to everyone. But it was doubly so to me, because, in addition to the awfulness of the event, my lifelong mind-set and beliefs had been knocked over. I knew that Nick's story was, quite simply, the truth, and that Nicholas really was occupying his mind.

"A few days after the president's assassination Nick and Nicholas came for their second session. It was during this session that Nick reported that Nicholas's voice was beginning to fade, and Nicholas himself said that he thought that he was leaving Nick's head. He had actually warned Nick a few days previously that he thought this was going to happen. Nick's response to this at that time has remained etched on my mind ever since. He said, 'Nicholas, you're not to say that. Never, never, never say that again. I want you to stay with me for ever. You are the wonderful, beautiful father I never had.' So, in a few short weeks, Nick had changed from being part of a hideous nightmare to discovering a loving father figure for the first time in his life. When Nicholas finally left Nick's head during the second session he suffered a profound bereavement.

I continued to work with him once a week for the rest of that term, continuing with the work that Nicholas had started. Some credit should go to Nicholas and to me. But more important than anything else was Nick's fierce determination to combat the legacy left to him by his parents. The triumphant result is the man sitting there. I believe, Kristin, that you have discovered that triumph for yourself.

Nick looked at Kristin and saw that tears were pouring. They both jumped up at the same time and fell into each other's arms. Alex and Jenny made a discreet exit.

"My poor darling, beautiful man. I love you so very much."

"I hope that means that you believe our story."

"Of course I do. And I can see why you found it so difficult to tell me. But you found the perfect way to do it."

Jenny came out and said, "Lunch will be ready in half an hour. Why don't you two take a walk round the garden?" They strolled out across the lawn, hand in hand, while Jenny beamed at them.

"What do you think happened to Nicholas when he left your head?"

"I really don't know. I often imagine that he is still out there keeping an eye on things. If he is, I would love to think he is pleased with the way things are going for me."

"How could he not be pleased? You have achieved so much. I have known that you are a strong person from day one. But I hadn't realised just how strong you are until I heard your astonishing story this morning."

"When Nicholas told me he thought he would soon be leaving me, and I asked him where he would be going to, he said that he assumed that he would be dead. He believed that his body must have died when his mind went back in time, so there was nowhere left for his mind to go. But I'm not sure he was right about that. I really hope that he is enjoying his retirement in a later time than August 2013. After all, when he left me there is no reason why he couldn't have returned to his body at the very same instant that he had left it, is there?"

"I guess not. But when we reach retirement ourselves, we can go to Poynings and find out."

There was a long pause. "Kristin, do you realise what you just said?"

"Yes, I said perhaps you two will be able to get together again sometime after August 2013."

"No! No! You said, 'When we reach retirement ourselves.' That means that you really hope and intend that we should stay together….for….for all our life."

"Yes it does doesn't it?" said Kristin, with her enchanting smile.

"I've been fantasising about that for weeks now. But I never dared imagine that you would want it?"

"What, you mean because you are such a hopeless, miserable, unlovable creature?" she asked – still smiling Nick noticed with relief.

"Yes, something like that. Kristin, will you marry me?"

"Well, I think I'd better. It will give me more time to convince you that you are actually an amazing, clever, strong, sensitive, intuitive and utterly gorgeous person."

Nick could think of nothing he could say to that, so he kissed her instead.

"Do you mind if we tell Alex & Jenny?"

"I'd like that. You tell them when we go in for lunch. I hope they'll be pleased."

"Don't worry Kristin. I *know* they will."

When they were sitting down at the table, Nick said, "We have something to tell you." He noticed that Jenny's jaw had dropped. "Kristin and I are engaged to be married."

Jenny gave a little shriek and rushed round the table to give them each a big hug and a kiss. Alex rushed out of the room saying, "I'll be back in a mo." He returned carrying a bottle of champagne. "We always keep one of these in the back of the fridge in case occasion crops up which deserves its attention."

"What better occasion could there be?" said Jenny.

After much toasting, leaving an empty bottle, Jenny said, "When will the wedding be?"

"We have no idea. We only got engaged twenty minutes ago in your beautiful garden," said Nick.

"Kristin, dear, why don't you use our phone after lunch to ring your parents to give them the happy news?"

"That's very generous of you. But I think Nick and I need to make some basic decisions first. Perhaps later in the afternoon, if that's OK."

"Of course. That sounds like a good idea."

§

"Well, what do you think?" Kristin asked.

"I think we should get our degrees first. I'm not sure why I think that. What do *you* think?"

"I agree with you. I'm sure you're right. I think it's because we both know that we won't be ready for something so hugely important as marriage before we have finished our degrees. I also think that, for the time being we should keep our engagement just between the four of us. How does that sound to you?"

"Yes, I'm happy with that. But you are going to tell your parents, aren't you?"

"I'm not sure about that any more. Not yet. Maybe at Christmas."

Both were feeling that perhaps they had been a little hasty.

§

Alex and Jenny joined them. "Are you ready to make that phone call?" asked Jenny.

"We've talked it over and decided that it would make sense for us to postpone the wedding until we have finished our degrees. So I won't ring my parents just yet. But thank you so much for the offer."

"Just remember that the offer is still open at whatever stage you decide that you would like to ring them."

"Jenny and I have been talking about your idea of finding digs during the vacs and getting temporary jobs," Alex said, "We really don't think this would be very practical. Even getting a bed-sit is quite expensive, and you have to give the landlord key-money up front before you can move in. Now, I don't know, but I would imagine that you don't have any income beyond your scholarship, which only covers term time."

"You're quite right I don't have any income. But I will when I've got a job. And I'm sure I can borrow from someone for the up-front costs."

"The point is, Nick, that we've had a better idea," said Alex. "We would love it if you will agree to live here throughout the vacations."

"It won't cost you a penny and we would love to look after you," Jenny added.

Nick was amazed. "You are such lovely, generous people. But I don't really think I can do that."

"Why ever not?" asked Alex.

"Well it just wouldn't be right. You've given me so much already – given me my life really. Don't you agree it wouldn't be right, Kristin?"

Kristin was not sure how to answer this. "I neither agree nor disagree. I want to stay right out of this. I'm sorry Nick, but it has to be decided between you three." She wasn't at all sure that she should have said that. She felt very uncomfortable about being there during this conversation.

"If I take you up on your generous offer, I will still get a job and pay you rent. That would be only right."

"We don't want any rent, you silly boy...."

Alex interrupted. "No Jenny, I think it's important that we respect his wishes on this. Of course, we don't *need* the rent. I can understand, Nick, that you feel it's important to pay your way. But, I would like you to agree that if, for any reason, you can't get a job that you would be comfortable doing, then you will live here rent-free. Do we have a deal?"

Nick hesitated. "We have a deal. And thank you both so very much. One of the reasons I feel slightly uncomfortable about it is that I can imagine many people would say that I should go back to Lewes in the vacs. But, I *won't* do that ever again."

§

That evening, when Kristin was on her own again, in her room at college, she felt she had a lot of thinking to do. She was confused and overwhelmed. It was the most dramatic day of her life, and she wanted to try to get her head round everything that had happened. First there was that completely ridiculous and impossible story. That seemed like the only way to describe it; it was straight out of a science fiction book. And yet, she also knew beyond any doubt that it was true. What possible reason could Alex have for lying? He seemed to Kristin to be a rather wonderful guy, with great integrity. Given that, the Kennedy prediction proved the reality of Nicholas. But she was not sure how she could properly digest the enormity of it all.

She already knew that Nick had had a tough life, but to live through the whole Nicholas experience and come through it with even more strength than he had already was simply astonishing. She was in awe of him, and it was certainly part of why she loved him.

And to cap it all, they were now engaged to be married. How on earth did that happen? She cast her mind back to the moment in the garden when she had said that thing about going to Poynings together when they were retired. She hadn't really thought properly about the implication of what she was saying. And her beautiful Nick had picked up on it and proposed to her, and she had accepted. It had all slipped by like a dream – a dream from which she was now awakening and feeling very uncertain. Echoes of Barley's talk of lame ducks were creeping into her head. Would she be able to cope with Nick – to give him everything he needed?

The only thing she knew with any certainty was that she loved him, and she was almost certain that he loved her.

Anyway, they now had almost three years to decide if they really wanted to get married.

§

The next few weeks were wrapped in a rosy glow for Nick and Kristin. Yet, for both of them there was also an edge of anxiety. Nick worried about how he could spend as much time with Kristin as he desperately wanted, and not lose sight of the overwhelming purpose of his life. He simply had to obtain a first class honours degree. There was really no question about this. To do this required a great many hours of hard work. As a result, he found he was often having to prevent himself from getting in touch with Kristin when he was desperate to do so.

This worried Kristin. Why did Nick have to work so very hard? It was not as if it was a struggle for him to learn and understand the work they were doing. Indeed, he seemed to keep up with it all rather more easily than she did. Nick seemed to be driven by some urgent need to acquire greater and greater understanding of their subject. What was driving him so hard that even she could vicariously feel the pressure of it? So how painful, she asked herself, must it be for poor, vulnerable Nick? He was very strong, she knew that. But was he risking pushing himself beyond even his high limits? And why? What was this remorseless drive all about?

Finally, one Friday afternoon, she decided that she must sort this out with Nick. She strode to his room, knocked peremptorily on the door and went in. "Nick, I'm sorry to interrupt you, but I feel I must. We need to spend some quality time together; we have some talking to do. We are both going to take the whole day off tomorrow, and you are going to take me to Ely for the day. I'm told it is a beautiful city."

Nick felt as if something had hit him. He had never seen Kristin like this; it was overwhelming. He hugged her fiercely to him. "Of course I will. I'm sorry, my darling. I've been neglecting you, haven't I?"

"No, I think you may be neglecting *us*. But I don't really understand why."

"I'm so sorry. I promise we'll get it all sorted out tomorrow. I love you so much, darling one."

"Do you? I had begun to think I was losing you."

§

Nick and Kristin got off the train at Ely. Nick had a tourist map of Ely with him. "What would you like to see here first?"

"I don't want to see anything until we have found somewhere to sit down and do some talking."

They wandered away from the station and found a signpost saying 'To the Riverside'. They followed the sign and found a bench beside the river.

"You and I know each other pretty well now, wouldn't you say?" asked Kristin.

"We certainly do."

"Right. But I'm puzzled that there is something very important to you that you are holding back – that you aren't telling me."

Nick looked shocked. "I don't understand. I've no idea what you are talking about. Oh Kristin, this is awful. Help me out. Please give me a clue as to what makes you feel that. I can't bear it that you think I'm holding out on you."

"OK!" She paused to think. "You and I are doing the same degree course. We both badly want to get a decent degree at the end of it so that we can get interesting and challenging jobs which will give us a decent income. I am reasonably confident of doing this and I'm not finding it too much of a struggle to keep up with it all. Now, I know that I am nowhere near as brainy as you are. And that's fine with me. It's just part of the man I love. So why is it that you feel you need to work for many hours longer than I do? We hardly see anything of each other – it's as if we were just casual acquaintances. It seems as if there is some hidden demon driving you remorselessly into more and more study. Why? Why? Why? You could get a better grade in your degree than I will without even trying. What aren't you telling me, Nick? Why are you so driven? What is it that you want to do with your life that requires such sky-high intellectual standards?" Her face crumpled, and she sobbed.

Nick hugged Kristin to him. After a while he said, "Oh, my poor, darling, gorgeous Kristin! I'm so very sorry. I realise now what it is we haven't talked about. I didn't make any conscious decision not to tell you. I suppose it was simply that, to me, it was so much of an obvious 'given' that you would know and understand it in the same unspoken way that I did. But I now see. Why should you? It isn't written on your soul as it is, inevitably, on mine. You see, I am the only person in the entire world who knows from direct personal experience that time travel exists – who knows that it has happened. To me it isn't just a theoretical possibility. It IS. But not only that. The fact that I had that direct experience is the *only* reason that I am not leading the lonely, miserable and utterly friendless existence that was poor Nicholas's fate. So, because of all this, I am driven, as you say, to use my life to do everything I can to uncover the secrets of time travel. The only way to reach this is through quantum mechanics, as has been well demonstrated already by Hugh Everett and Richard Feynman. To end up with some kind of research job or professorship in quantum mechanics will need nothing less than a first class honours degree. That is the only thing I can think of that I haven't told you. As I say, it wasn't a secret. It just didn't occur to me, I don't know why. I'm so sorry."

There was a long silence while Kristin digested this. Finally she said, "I'm sorry too, Nick my darling. I was being rather dense not to realise what this was about. I can completely see now, and understand, the strength of this drive. The trouble with a drive like that is that you can *never* do enough; it will always seem to you that you urgently need to do more than you are doing at present. In the end even a tough old nut like you will break. What good will that do?"

"I don't know what to think."

"Oh, my poor, driven boy. I believe a big part of our problem is that you don't give yourself enough credit. Old habits I suppose. Think about it: You qualified for a Trinity scholarship, you left school with four – yes, four – A grades at A Level. How many people do you know who have achieved all that?....Go on, how many?"

"Well I don't think I know any. But I'm sure there are several at Cambridge."

"I rest my case. I would say that the only chance of you not getting a first is if you carry on as you are now. You will more than likely burn yourself out. In addition to that, *I* can't cope with any more of it. If you carry on as you are now we will have to stop seeing each other altogether. It will be over for us. I mean that Nick."

"Yes, sweetheart, I know you do. And I'm not even saying you're wrong about the risk of burn-out. There is a risk; I'm conscious of it."

"So I'll tell you my terms," Kristin said with a grin. "We must have two evenings a week together and all day on Sundays. Agreed?"

"Of course, Kristin, of course. And thank you for not giving up on me. I love you so much."

"Me too. Now, come on, let's go and see Ely."

Map in hand, Nick led her along a lane beside The Cutter Inn. They crossed another road and went between some wrought iron gates on to a large green. On the far side was the cathedral, standing out against a blue sky scattered with white, fluffy clouds. They walked into this amazing building, and wandered up the nave until, looking up, they could see the astonishing site of the octagon tower seeming to float unsupported over their heads, sunshine pouring in through its windows.

"I never knew such a building could exist," said Nick.

"It certainly is very special," replied Kristin. "But have you never seen any other cathedrals."

"No, never!"

"How come?"

"Mother and father never took us on outings. And since then, I haven't really had any motivation to go on my own. I suppose it has just never occurred to me that it would be worth doing....Until now."

During their remaining time at Cambridge, Nick kept his agreement, and his and Kristin's love for each other became even stronger, but also more comfortable, closer but less frenzied. They got to know each other's friends and increasingly felt immersed in love and friendship. They both felt and delighted in the wonder of this.

Sometimes Nick would ask Kristin, in genuine puzzlement, why on earth she loved him so much. She would say that she loved his strength as well as his gentleness, his braininess as well as his compassion for others, and his extraordinary ability to work out what was troubling people who were being unkind. She would tell him he was not only good looking, but also had an amazing interior beauty which quite overwhelmed her at times. Then Nick would tell her of all the reasons he loved her. Of the time when he first saw her – a beautiful flower in a stony wilderness; of her wisdom and kindness; of her amazing patience; of her ability to look at things from many angles; of her loyalty and of her insights into other people's troubles; and, of course, of her amazing sexiness.

Nick continued with his rowing and managed to get a place in the Trinity first eight. This was the only organised extra-curricular activity he allowed himself. He was still very driven, but, with Kristin's understanding support, he was able to keep it much more under control.

§

Kristin was very keen for Nick to spend the long summer vac with her and her family in Cologne. But she knew that he was always more or less penniless. So she wrote to her mum to say that term ended on Friday, 13th June, and would it be OK for Nick to stay for the vacation? Also, could they possibly pay for Nick's return fare because he had very little money?

Ten days later Kristin received a reply from her mum to say that she and dad were really looking forward to meeting Nick, having heard so much about this remarkable young man. She had enclosed two airline tickets for a flight from Heathrow to Cologne/Bonn departing on the afternoon of the 14th. Her parents really were a bit special thought Kristin. She hadn't mentioned her plan to Nick yet, knowing that he would resist the idea of her parents paying for him to come out. But if it was a *fait accompli*....!

"Nick, have you got anything planned for the vac?"

"Well I will be doing my usual vac job in Heffers book shop."

"The thing is that my mum and dad have invited you to spend the vac with them in Cologne. It would be wonderful to be together for the whole of the vac."

"I would love that, but I can't. I haven't got any money, and it must cost a fortune to travel there."

"It's not a problem. With the letter inviting you they included two air tickets."

"But I can't ask them to....."

"You don't need to ask them anything, darling. They've already done it."

"I don't know what to say. It will be so wonderful."

They hugged each other with delight. 'God you're a devious cow,' thought Kristin, grinning, 'but it's all in a good cause.'

"All we have to do now is get you a passport. Don't worry," Kristin said as Nick showed signs of protest. "I'll pay for it. I've got plenty of emergency funds, and this is definitely an emergency."

Nick wondered at her. She seemed to know about everything; she was a world citizen.

# Chapter 17

By the time they got to Heathrow, Nick and Kristin were both feverishly excited. Nick's head was whirling – so many people, so many signs and notices, it was a frenzy. He had no idea what he was supposed to do or where they had to go. Fortunately Kristin seemed to know what she was doing.

"Do you normally fly to and from Cologne?" Nick asked.

"I have done a couple of times, but normally I go by sea and train. This time it was entirely mum and dad's idea."

Nick had to admit, to himself that he was scared of this whole flying thing. After all, there were regular accounts in the papers and on TV of awful crashes. When their aircraft's engines suddenly rose to a roar and he could feel the extraordinary pressure pushing him into the back of his seat, he panicked and grabbed Kristin's hand. Nick and Kristin looked at each other. She looked into his eyes and could see the terror. Nick half expected her to laugh at him, but she just squeezed his hand and said, "This bit will be over very soon." Nick felt ashamed, but also almost overwhelmed by his beloved's compassion. This feeling, unique to him in his entire life, he retained and treasured for the rest of it.

When they had left the plane at Cologne/Bonn airport, Nick heaved a sigh of relief. They collected their baggage and trundled into the arrivals hall. Kristin was surprised to see a guy holding up a card with her name on it. She walked over to him, puzzled, "Hullo, I'm Kristin Bruchner."

"I am a taxi driver. I have instructions to take you and your friend to Rodenkirchen. It's all paid for."

"Oh, that's great. Thank you."

The taxi driver took the baggage trolley and loaded its contents into the boot of his taxi. Kristin explained to Nick, "Good old Mum! She's arranged for this taxi to take us home. Well it may have been Dad, but it sounds more like Mum to me."

Nick looked around in amazement during the drive. "This is such a beautiful city. I'm amazed," he said.

"Why are you amazed?" Kristin asked.

"Well I presumed that it must have been badly damaged during the war."

"It certainly was. The whole of the central area was completely flattened. Apparently one of the architects of the new city described it as the world's largest heap of rubble. There are those who say that it is the beautiful city we can see today precisely because the town planners and architects had the chance to start again from scratch."

They crossed a bridge over the River Rhine, and on the far side the taxi turned left off the main road. Kristin said, "This is Rodenkirchen which is a sort of suburb of Cologne. It's where we live. Mum and dad will both be at work, but I've got a key."

Soon the taxi turned in to a drive leading up to what Nick thought was a huge house. The taxi driver took their luggage to the front door while Kristin used her key to open up. She cancelled the beeping of the alarm, and they carried their luggage in. Kristin led the way upstairs and into a huge bedroom with an enormous double bed. "Let's get the unpacking done now," Kristin said. "You can have that chest-of-drawers and I'll have this one."

"But….I mean….Are we both going to…."

"Of course. Don't you want to?"

"Oh, my God! Of course, but what will your parents think?

"Mum, wrote to me a couple of weeks ago to ask if we wanted one bedroom or two. So....here we are." Kristin's adorable, impish smile shone like a beacon. Nick rushed to her, overflowing with adoration. The unpacking was postponed for a while.

§

The front door banged and a girl's voice called out. Kristin pulled Nick out to the hall. A teenage girl stood there jigging up and down with excitement and grinning like a Cheshire cat. Kristin hugged her and said, "Anneliese, this is Nick, my *fiancé*." She emphasised the word extravagantly. Anneliese shook Nick's hand. "You are a very lucky man." She blushed, confused. "And, of course, Kristin is very lucky too." Overcome by embarrassment, she rushed off to her room.

Kristin laughed. "Anneliese is my sister. She's fifteen, and does get herself into a muddle when boys are present."

Nick laughed. "What about your brother; has he flown the nest?"

"Yes, he is a solicitor, which pleases dad no end, and he lives with his wife in West Berlin."

When Gisela Bruchner came home, Kristin was in the hall waiting to welcome her. She was a slim, smartly dressed woman with straight, blond hair just like Kristin's. She also had Kristin's open and sunny smile. They hugged each other. "Welcome back home again darling. Have you had a good term?"

"Wonderful, thanks Mum." They both grinned.

"But I hope you're keeping up with your degree work?"

"Yes, it's all going well."

"Well come on then," Gisela said in a conspiratorial voice. "Where is he? Where is he?"

"He's outside admiring your garden."

They hurried out and found Nick standing by the pond. "Hullo, Nick, welcome to our home. I'm Gisela, Kristin's mother. She has told me very much about you, and I have been so much looking forward to this moment."

"It is wonderful to meet you, too. You two look so like each other. You have the most beautiful house and garden I have ever seen."

"Thank you Nick." She turned to Kristin. "You have a very polite young man there."

Gisela took Nick's arm and walked him round her beloved garden pointing out the highlights.

§

Later, Nick was introduced to Kasper Bruchner, Kristin's father. "How do you do, sir. I am very pleased to meet you." He was a heavily built man with slightly greying hair and a neat moustache. Nick thought he looked as if he had once been a rugby player.

"How do you do, Nick. Very welcome," he said with a heavy German accent. He turned to Gisela and said something in German.

Gisela said, "Kasper asked me to apologise that he does not speak any English. He has been looking forward to meeting you every bit as much as I have."

That evening after dinner they went into the sitting room and, what Nick thought of as the inquisition, began. There were rather a lot of areas which he didn't want to talk about — his family, his therapy with Alex, and obviously nothing about Nicholas. He was very nervous.

"I believe you are doing a natural sciences degree as well, is that right?" asked Gisela.

"Yes, and we are both at Trinity, and we are both in the same year."

Kristin added, "So you see we were destined for each other."

The conversation didn't flow as easily as it might as everything said to or by Kasper had to be translated. But Nick felt it eased the pressure a little.

"I know from her letters that Kristin is enjoying the course. Are you enjoying it as well, Nick?"

"Yes, very much. But it's quite tough – a steep learning curve."

"Kristin tells me that you work extremely hard at it and put in a lot of hours."

Nick felt uncomfortable. "Well yes, I suppose I do. But Kristin and I have come to an agreement about our together time." Nick wondered if perhaps he shouldn't have said that. Kasper said something in German. Now Kristin looked uncomfortable.

"Kasper says there is nothing at all wrong with hard work; great rewards flow from it. He hopes that we are not too much of a distraction to each other."

"There's no need for either of you to worry," said Kristin. "We are both going to get our degrees." Then she spoke to her dad in German, presumably reassuring him as well, Nick thought.

"Do you have a big family, Nick? Where do you live?"

"Just my parents and an older brother who is in the army now. My parents live in Lewes near the south coast."

Gisela looked puzzled and Kristin quickly intervened in German to translate for her father. Then she hastily added in English, "Nick has always been a keen hiker, and we've been out walking together in Cambridgeshire. It's infectious; I'm learning to love it too."

"What about school, Nick? What sort of school did you attend?"

"I went to a boarding school in Lincolnshire, about fifty miles north of Cambridge."

"A boarding school? That sounds rather tough."

"No, no, I loved it. The quality of the teaching was very good and I have always liked the academic life."

Kasper asked him something, which was translated as "Do you have any ideas about your career after you have got your degree?"

"Yes, definitely! I want to get some sort of research job in the area of quantum physics."

Kristin held Nick's hand and translated for him, "That sounds very impressive. Is there much demand for that sort of thing? What prompts you to go for that?"

This was all going exactly the way Nick had hoped it wouldn't. "I just think it's a fascinating area. And it's right on the frontiers of physics."

When at last they were alone together in their bedroom, Kristin said, "Oh you poor man, Nick. I hope that wasn't too awful."

"Well it did get a bit close to stuff I really didn't want to talk about, but I think I came out of it as something a little better than an ogre."

"You were a star. Before I came up here I had a quick chat with mum in the kitchen. They both think you are a *wunderkind.*"

"What's that mean?"

"Well it normally translates as 'child prodigy'. But in this case they mean something like 'superman'". They both laughed, but Kristin said, "They're absolutely right. Now let's go to bed and you can show me what you can do, Superman."

§

Thus began a fifteen week idyll for Kristin and Nick. Kristin guided Nick round every inch of Cologne taking in many museums and galleries. They particularly enjoyed the Forstbotanischer Garten – an amazing botanic garden specialising in trees. It was walking distance from the Bruchners' house and they visited it three times, spending many hours in this beautiful place. In July, Gisela and Kasper treated them to three weeks of walking in the Black Forest, staying at farmhouse accommodation.

When this summer of delight finally drew to a close, and Cambridge beckoned, Nick and Kristin felt sad that it was ending, but happy that they would be able for ever to remember this perfect period in their lives when they first truly became one. Nick was effusive in his thanks to Gisela and Kasper, saying that he had never known such kindness and generosity in his entire life. Gisela had the sad feeling that this was probably true. Poor, dear Nick. But she knew that Kristin would take care of him and cherish him.

# Chapter 18

For the next two years Nick & Kristin both worked very hard. Kristin was also now thinking that maybe an honours degree could be within her grasp. Nevertheless, they stuck to their together time agreement, and twice a month went to Alex and Jenny's for Sunday lunch. It was only in their final term at Trinity that they both accepted that their agreement should be abandoned in the final push to their degrees.

Kristin achieved a Second, and Nick a starred First. They celebrated with their friends for several days. At no time in this period were any of them entirely sober. It was on day three that Nick and Kristin had to sit down and say 'OK, done that, what's next?' They both agreed that top of the list was their marriage. "I know my mum and dad would love it if we were to get married in Cologne. How would you feel about that Nick? Would you mind very much?"

"Of course not, that would be wonderful. There is no-one in England that I want to invite, apart from Alex and Jenny, of course. And perhaps one or two of our university friends."

"But surely, Nick, you'll be inviting your parents and Jeremy, won't you?"

"Absolutely not! Please, don't let's go there, Kristin. I won't do that."

"That's OK darling, I understand. Then we need to think about getting a job. I think I would like to look for one in the research department of some large corporation. How about that, Nick. It would be great if we could work for the same company."

"Well, it couldn't be straight away. I'll need three years to get my PhD. Professor Jade has given me the names of several possible sources of funding for it. He says that with a first there will be no difficulty in getting funding. But, of course, if it's a corporation it would almost certainly mean that I would have to work for them for a certain number years after obtaining the PhD."

The blood had drained from Kristin's face, but, in his enthusiasm Nick didn't notice. "And where do I fit into this grand design," Kristin asked icily.

Nick look bemused. "Well I'm sure there are plenty of job opportunities in Cambridge for a highly qualified person like you."

"So, we rent a little flat in Cambridge, and I get a job in some accountant's office. If you think that is what I have spent all these years of seriously hard study for, Nick Harrison, then you're an insensitive dolt."

"Oh, that's not fair. You have known all along what has been driving me. I must be able to do research into time travel. You know why that is. And you agreed to it."

"I never agreed to your following up your degree with another three years of intensive study while you get a doctorate, during which time I have a rubbish job and we hardly see anything of each other."

"I can't get into the sort of research work I need without a doctorate, and I'm sure you must have realised this."

"Fuck you, Nick. I love you. God knows why, but I do. Even so, I'm not giving up everything I'm owed for *my* hard work, so that you can follow your grotesque obsession to go chasing after Nicholas through time. I'm going. Do not follow me."

She ran back to her room and collapsed on her bed crying and sobbing. Why on earth didn't she see this coming? Probably because she didn't want to see it. It suddenly all seemed rather predictable. Oh God, why did she let herself fall in love with such a sad, damaged man. But she did love him. Tough! Get over it! The wedding is cancelled and there's an end to it.

When Kristin left, Nick felt as if he had been kicked by a horse. He was finding it difficult to breath. What on earth happened there? What had come over her? She had known almost since they first met that he needed to work in quantum physics to see if he could find the foundation of what happened to Nicholas. And she understood this need; at least, he thought she had. But perhaps she had simply dumped him because she had suddenly seen through him and realised he was a no-hope, defective human being. Eventually he cried himself to sleep.

He woke at seven the next morning and got out of bed. He saw that a note had been pushed under the door, and the whole horror of yesterday evening crashed into his head. He grabbed the note and read it.

*Dear Nick,*

*I have left Cambridge. I am going back home. Don't follow me. There will be no wedding. I love you. But I can't cope with your obsession. I'm sorry. I should be better than that. But I'm not. I will miss you. Have a good life.*

*Kristin.*

§

Next morning Nick was slumped at his desk, apathetic and lost in despair. He didn't know what to do. He was too lost to climb out of the pit.

There came a knock at the door. Alex came in. "The porter showed me where to come." He grabbed the other chair, sat down by Nick and took his hand. "Gisela Bruchner phoned me half an hour ago. She sounded very distressed, but I gathered Kristin has left you. That's all I know. Do you want to fill me in?"

Nick said nothing. Alex waited in silence. After five minutes or so Nick struggled haltingly to tell Alex everything. It was very painful and difficult, but he owed Alex, of all people, as much explanation as he could. "Thank you for that, Nick. It can't have been easy. What I want you to do now is to pack up your things. You've got to be out of the room by the end of the day anyway.

"Then you're coming home to stay with Jenny and me. Where's your luggage? You pass things to me and I will pack them."

On the way back to his house Alex said, "When Mrs Bruchner rang she said she would ring again this evening. She asked if I might be able to arrange for you to be in the house then, so that you and she could talk together."

"Did she sound angry?"

"No, she sounded distressed and worried, but I couldn't detect any anger there."

When they got to the house Alex said, "What I suggest is that you take your stuff up to your room and then go and have a long soak in the bath. Then, when you're ready, I'll make us some breakfast and we will have a long talk."

Nick threw his arms round Alex, saying, "I don't know why you are so good to me, especially when I don't deserve it."

"Get away! Go and get in that bath."

After breakfast, they took their coffee out on to the veranda. "Jenny's away for the day, but she was still here when Kristin's mother rang, so she knows roughly what has happened. She asked me to give you her love, and she says she will be thinking of you and Kristin. She will be back this evening. But I believe it's just as well that it's only you and me here today. You're used to telling me everything on your mind."

"Yes, I suppose so. But I don't think any amount of talking is going to change anything."

"Perhaps so, perhaps not! You said earlier that you didn't think you deserved any sympathy. Why's that?"

"Because I've hurt Kristin so dreadfully, and it was through pure selfishness. We were talking about what we wanted to do next, and she had very reasonably said that she would like to get a job working in the research labs of a large company, and maybe we could work for the same company. It was a very reasonable and sensible idea. So what did I do? I blared out that I couldn't leave Cambridge for another three years because I had to get a PhD. I want this; I want that; me, me, me! And my plans were in total conflict with hers. She couldn't possibly find a suitable job in Cambridge. But what did I say then? – That I was sure that with her qualifications she could find a job in Cambridge. How patronising can anyone get? *I* was looking for a career not a job. So was she. But I suggested that she found a *job* so as to fit with *my* career." Nick was almost shouting – in rage and self-flagellation.

"But that isn't the worst of it. My wonderful, high priority career which required Kristin to take a back seat isn't even a career, it's an obsession. An obsession that requires the world to grant me the privilege of discovering the science of time travel. And do you know? It was at that final, terrible row that Kristin, for the first time, used the word 'obsession' to describe my ambitions, even though I am sure she had thought it many times before. Dear Kristin, so gentle, so tactful. And now I have destroyed it all utterly and for ever."

"Are you sure about that? Why do you think Gisela is phoning you this evening?"

"I don't know. Probably to tell me what a bastard I am."

"How did she get my phone number, do you think?"

"Kristin must have told her."

"What does that tell you?"

"Nothing really. Perhaps she wanted her mum to tell me I'm a bastard."

"Or?"

"Yeah, yeah!" Nick showed the smallest of smiles. "Because Kristin wanted her mother to maintain some sort of contact. I wish I was able to believe that."

"This evening will tell." They sat in silence for a while.

"You know, there is something else I've realised since Kristin left. For years I have believed that my plan – no, my destiny – to discover how people can travel back in time was based on the strongest evidence – namely that Nicholas had already done it. But he hadn't set out to do it. He was as staggered as I was when it happened. So the whole Nicholas saga doesn't provide the slightest evidence that man can deliberately manipulate time in any way. So the whole passion I had which caused me to slap Kristin in the face was based on nothing. I could not be more ashamed if I tried."

That evening everyone's nerves were on edge. Jenny kept picking up her knitting, making a few stitches and then putting it down again. Alex prowled about the house. And Nick kept imagining all the many different things that Gisela might say.

The phone rang. All three jumped. Alex rushed to the phone.

"Alex Henderson."

"Mr Henderson, good evening. It's Gisela Bruchner. Is Nick with you now?"

"Yes, I'll call him."

Nick lurched to the phone; he was shaking all over. "Hello Gisela. Thank you so much for ringing."

Gisela could hear the shaking in his voice. "Oh, you poor, poor boy. What have you two been up to?"

"How's Kristin? Is she all right?"

"Far from it. She thinks she has lost you. She is distraught."

"Oh my God! Can I talk to her?"

"No Nick, I'm afraid you can't. She says she can't talk to you on the phone; it has to be face to face." Nick's heart leapt.

"So I have this morning put an open dated airline ticket in the post to you."

"Oh, Gisela, you are wonderful. Thank you so much. I will pay for the ticket as soon as I can."

"You will indeed, in the only way you can repay me. You two must sort yourselves out. I have never known two people so meant for each other. Now I've got a wedding to organise."

§

When Nick reached the arrivals hall at Cologne/Bonn airport he soon spotted a white sign saying 'Nick Harrison'. It seemed to Nick that the journey to the house took for ever this time. But eventually the taxi got there.

As he gathered up his luggage, Gisela hurried out. "Nick, it's lovely to see you. Kristin's in the garden."

Nick dropped his luggage in the hall, and walked out into the garden. His heart was pounding. When he saw Kristin he was shocked. She looked wretched – as if she had just witnessed a violent and horrifying scene.

"Hi Kristin!" He didn't know what else to say without a cue from Kristin. Had Kristin's mum perhaps forced this meeting against her wishes? 'Please say something Kristin,' he thought.

"I imagine mum has been giving you the whole script – 'it's all a lot of fuss about nothing. Just get it sorted out' – and so on."

"Yes, that sort of thing."

"Well we certainly need to do some talking. I didn't want to do it on the phone; that would have been ghastly and useless. So here we are, face to face. We may still be parting at the end of this, but at least we will have done some proper communicating, I hope, and not just that awful, screaming fight. Nick can you please set the ball rolling by telling me what you have been feeling and thinking since then?"

This was so weird, Nick thought. This wasn't Kristin, talking in this strange, stilted way. It sounded as if she was reporting something to a committee. He couldn't bear to hear much more of it.

"What have I been feeling? How to put that in words?" He paused. "It was as if everything I loved in the world had been snatched away. As if all colour had gone and everything looked a dirty sepia. I have never yet suffered a bereavement, but it could not possibly be more tragic, or a greater loss than what I was feeling. And then I felt utterly ashamed of the way I had spoken to you and of the way I had not spared a moment to think of what you wanted and needed; ashamed of my total, thoughtless selfishness."

"Stop it Nick! You're just taking all the blame, and that's not right. I said some terrible things to you which I regret so much. You just didn't deserve them. If we were to stay together, the problem between us is actually very simply stated. The next steps in my career ambitions and yours are completely incompatible. That's what we need to resolve."

"I agree. So let me tell you what I have been thinking. You used the word 'obsession' to describe my future plans. Thinking about that afterwards, I realised that you were completely right. I have been obsessed with time travel ever since Nicholas left me. In all that time I have had tunnel vision; I was being forced very hard down that tunnel by the ghost of Nicholas. But thanks to you I now know that. When I added to that knowledge the fact that I had a simple choice – time travel research or Kristin....Well, to use one of Nicholas's phrases, it was a no-brainer. I have no wish to do any postgraduate study. I no longer have any specific ambitions other than to spend the rest of my life with you, if you will allow this."

Kristin put her arms round Nick's neck and kissed him. "Let's pretend that horrible row never happened, shall we?"

"What horrible row?" Nick grinned. "We'd better go inside and tell your mum that the wedding's back on again so that she can carry on where she left off."

Hand in hand they walked indoors.

Later that day Kristin found the opportunity to sit down and do some thinking. When Nick first revealed, on that dreadful day, his plans to pursue a doctorate, she was quite overwhelmed with anger. She still felt that this was very natural and understandable, particularly as Nick did not seem to have given a moment's consideration to *her* career needs. But she needn't have let her feelings boil over so fast. She should have had more self-control, allowing them to talk it through properly. And what must Nick have felt when he read that awful note she put under the door? He really didn't deserve that, poor man.

At the time, she was distraught with a mixture of anger, despair, grief and panic. It felt, she thought, as if she was going mad. As soon as she had put the note under Nick's door, she threw all her belongings into a case and got a taxi to the station. That was the start of a journey of total nightmare. She went to Heathrow assuming that she would be able to get a ticket for a flight on the spot. She was very lucky; the airline had received a cancellation. Throughout the flight she churned everything over and over in her head. She finally got home at about 8:00pm, much to the surprise of her mother who had not been expecting her for another three days. Kristin told her the sorry tale. She said she had been impetuous and utterly stupid and, as a result, had lost the dearest person in her life. Her mother had been wonderful, and completely calm, helping her to sort out her feelings, and understand what had been happening to Nick and herself. Her mother had taken care of everything, and two days later Nick was on the doorstop.

The meeting in the garden, as it seemed to her now, happened in a misty haze. Nick was much too hard on himself. He was as entitled as she to have plans for a career. But he had capitulated completely. She had thought these things were supposed to end in compromise, and she felt this total reversal was not how it should be. But Nick, darling, lovely Nick, was very convincing that he fully understood her position. Not only that, he provided a good argument that his need to discover the secrets of time travel were absurd and doomed to fail.

She had got her Nick back, but she couldn't help feeling a little ashamed of her part in it.

# Chapter 19

Nick was amazed to find how complicated a business getting married in Germany was, especially if either or both parties were not German citizens. Because of this, Gisela and Kasper had decided on a date in early September for the wedding. Kristin made a small protest about not being consulted, but it was really only a token; she knew that she had no desire to do all the form filling and rushing about. Nick felt very uncomfortable about being "kept" by Gisela and Kasper all this time, and decided that he would try to look for a temporary job. Gisela pointed out that he would not be able to do that because he didn't have a work permit. Instead she suggested that he do a crash course in German; she and Kristin could help him. A friend of hers owned a language school; she would see what he could do for him. She also pointed out that being able to speak German would greatly increase his chances of finding the perfect career. Nick started at the language school, and everyone was amazed at the progress he was making. He laconically suggested that he was just applying his customary obsessiveness.

Preparations for the wedding proceeded steadily, and at one point Nick had to return to England to sort out all the form filling required at that end. He had the chance to catch up with Alex and Jenny. He told them that the wedding would take place in Cologne, but the venue for the reception had not yet been decided. He asked Alex if he would be willing to be his best man. He said he was amazed to be asked, but joyfully accepted. He thought he would probably be the oldest best man in history.

The wedding finally took place on 10<sup>th</sup> September at the Cologne Register Office, and afterwards at a nearby hotel. As well as Alex and Jenny, five of Nick and Kristin's university friends flew over for the event. Impeccably organised as it was by Gisela, everything went very smoothly. Nick amazed everyone by talking in a very relaxed German to all the guests. Kristin was impressed not only by this but by how her shy Nick was getting on so well with many people he had never met before.

After a completely wonderful honeymoon – two weeks in Scotland, which neither of them had ever been to before – they returned to start work in the research department at a large pharmaceutical company in Dusseldorf, jobs that they had been interviewed for in early August. This was the start of careers which they both found were satisfying and rewarding. After three years, Kristin took an extended eighteen months maternity leave, with a promise that her job would be waiting for her when she returned. She gave birth to a little girl whom they christened Gretel Rose.

§

In 2009, when Nick and Kristin were 59, and had become devoted grandparents to Gretel's twins, they decided it was time for them to take early retirement. During their careers they had been able to put away considerable sums, and they both had very good pensions to come.

"Where would you like to retire to? Would you like to stay here?" asked Kristin.

"Well no, what I would really like is to retire to my beloved Sussex. Would you mind that, dear?"

"No, I wouldn't mind a bit. In fact, I had guessed you would probably say that. After all, there's nothing to keep us here. Sussex would be a wonderful place for Gretel, Berthold and the twins to come for holidays."

"But wouldn't you miss Germany badly?"

"Not at all. I feel as much English as German. Anyway I could always pop back whenever I wanted. Remember we're not going to be short of a pfennig or two."

"Thank you darling Kristin. You're always so good to me."

§

They rented a furnished flat in Hove while they looked for somewhere to buy. They had their furniture shipped across and put into storage. Nick went on line to register their details and requirements with all the estate agents that covered the South Downs area.

Soon, the details of houses started to clatter through their letter box. Life became a frenzy of driving round Sussex looking at one property after another. Perhaps they had been too detailed in their specifications, but nothing seemed to be just right.

One afternoon as they were driving along the A27 to go and have a look at a house in Shoreham, Nick spotted a signpost and turned off the main road to head north.

"This is the wrong road for Shoreham," said Kristin as Nick pulled into a layby.

"What's wrong Nick?" asked Kristin anxiously. Nick looked very pale and he was sweating. "Are you feeling unwell?"

"No, I'm fine. It was just something I saw on a signpost. Don't worry about it."

Kristin thought about this. "It was 'Poynings' you saw on the signpost wasn't it?"

"Yes. I'm sorry darling. I swore to myself that I would never think about it again. It was just that name which suddenly hit me."

"Of course you're going to think about it, my love. Especially now that you are in Sussex again. I've been thinking about it too."

"Do you realise it was just three weeks ago that Nicholas moved into his cottage. He should be there right now."

"God that's weird."

"Isn't it? Do you mind....I mean, shall we go and take a look? We needn't go in; just look from outside."

"I think we've got to, haven't we? It's too amazing to ignore. There might be two of you."

"I don't think I want to meet him. Apart from anything else, I think that would be impossible....or even dangerous."

"Let's go and look....just from a distance." Kristin seemed to be as drawn to it as Nick.

When they drove cautiously into the village, the first thing they saw was a 'For Sale' sign beside the gate to Nicholas's house.

"That doesn't make sense," Nick said. "He's only just moved in. Perhaps we can peer through a window."

"Let's be careful. You stay in the car. I'll go and look."

She walked up the path, feeling like an intruder. She looked through the window to the left of the front door. The room was empty – no furniture, no carpet, nothing. She hurried back to the car. "God, that was creepy. Quickly; drive on Nick."

When they got back to the flat, Nick made a pot of tea and they sat out on the balcony overlooking the sea.

"So, how do you explain that?" Kristin asked.

"I don't know that I can. But let's think it through. If time travel into the past exists – and we know that it does – then the only one of the current theories that could explain it is one of the parallel universe theories."

"Oh yes, right. And in that theory, every time anything changes in a universe, even something as small as the quantum shift of an electron, then the universe splits into two universes.

141

Both continue to co-exist – one in which the quantum shift has happened, and one in which it hasn't."

"Yes, and if that law applies to changes as small as a quantum shift, it certainly applies to much bigger changes, like someone going back in time to occupy his own head at an earlier age."

"So," said Kristin, "at the point in time where Nicholas entered you head, you and I and everyone else changed to a new universe. Even so, why isn't Nicholas at the house in Poynings? He hasn't gone back in time yet."

"Well I think that's because he is in Poynings in the old universe. The moment he jumped back in time, I was the only Nicholas in the new universe, with a sort of ghost of myself in my head for a while. I suspect that the reason we have difficulty in taking that on board is that we are stuck with the illusion that time really exists in the sense that it 'moves' from the past to the future via the present. I think the reality is an infinite set of parallel, branching histories, co-existing from the infinite past to the infinite future. There is no 'now' or 'yet' or 'then'."

"But doesn't that mean that everything is pre-ordained"

"I don't think it does. I think it simply means that when we make a choice to do one thing or another, we are reaching another divide in the time lines. We are choosing to be part of one universe rather than its parallel alternative."

§

The next morning, when Kristin was opening the post, she gasped. "Nick look". She held out an estate agent's property description. Nick took it.

"It's for Newtimber Cottage. Oh, that's weird!"

"Not really. We know the house is for sale. Perhaps the sign has only just gone up."

"What do you think?" asked Nick. He still wasn't really sure what Kristin thought about all this stuff.

"I think we should contact the estate agent and go and look at it."

When they reached Poynings at eleven o'clock as arranged, the girl from the estate agent was waiting for them. She took them in and showed them round. There was a massive living room stretching from front to back of the house; it was the one that Kristin had peered at through the window. It had large, modern windows on three sides, with fantastic views from all three. But the view from the back window was particularly fine, looking out at the wooded flank of Newtimber Hill. Across a small hall was a large kitchen/dining room with kitchen equipment which looked as if it was installed only yesterday. Upstairs were three bedrooms and a well-equipped bathroom. There was also an attic which was accessed by a sliding ladder.

The girl from the estate agents said, "I'll leave you to take it all in. I've unlocked the back door so that you can look round the garden. I'll be just outside in my car if you need anything."

Nick wandered all over the house as if in a dream. Kristin knew that if she said something to him now he probably wouldn't hear her. He was reliving some very important parts of his childhood, she thought, and this house must feel like part of him. She knew what they were going to do, and she was totally happy about it.

She followed him out into the garden. It seemed to Kristin like a garden made in heaven, very peaceful – and those views; nobody could ever tire of them.

Nick was looking into a substantial garden shed. "This must be where he made his model machines."

Not really, thought Kristin, that was in the other universe. But she knew better than to say anything.

"Nick, darling, let's buy this. Please!"

"I hope you're not just saying that because you know it's what I want."

"I absolutely love it. I can't wait to live in this beautiful house on these beautiful downs."

§

During the next few years Nick and Kristin had what they both regarded as an idyllic period in their lives. Kristin put her own stamp on Newtimber Cottage. They did all the painting and decorating themselves. Kristin became as passionate a downs-walker as Nick. They walked a great many of the downs footpaths together.

One evening in August 2013 as they sat in their cottage gazing out at the last bright sunshine on the crest of the hill, with the dark trees of Newtimber Wood below, Kristin knew that something was agitating Nick; she knew the signs too well. "What's up, Nick? You look worried."

"No, not worried, just rather weird. I have been thinking about tomorrow being August 13th."

Kristin waited to hear more, but Nick was silent and pensive. "Sorry, I'm not with you. What's special about August 13th?"

"It was on the night of 13th/14th that Nicholas left his body behind to enter my head."

Something twisted in Kristin's chest. She guessed that this must be lying heavily on her poor man's spirit. She took his hand and they sat in silence, each buried in their own anxieties.

Finally Nick said, "Will you come walking with me tomorrow? I want to retrace that first amazing walk that Nicholas and I did from Lewes to here."

"Of course I'll come with you darling. It's important to you that we should do it, isn't it?"

"Yes I suppose so, in a way. We could get the eight o'clock bus to Lewes and walk back."

§

Nick insisted that they buy food from the same Lewes bakers as last time, to take with them on the walk. As on the previous occasion, it was a beautiful day with wall-to-wall blue sky. Nick was delighted that they could still hear the larks, even though their numbers had apparently fallen drastically in recent years. They walked up the gentle slope of soft chalkland turf to the top of Blackcap.

"It was the first time I had ever seen a trig point. I had no idea what it was for. Nicholas explained the whole system to me brilliantly. He was such a good teacher. Way over there you can just see the start of The Seven Sisters at Cuckmere."

"Oh yes, you can can't you. You wouldn't be able to see it if it wasn't such a clear day."

"Just as it was last time…..Fifty years ago tomorrow."

Kristin gazed at Nick. He looked….stretched was the word that struck her. Was he suffering, or was he enjoying the surreal memories? A bit of both probably, she thought.

They continued the walk. "It was as we were walking along this stretch that we first learned how to talk to each other silently. This stopped people thinking I was talking to myself, but created even more of a problem, because we soon learned that when we were having these inward conversations, I was totally unaware of what was happening around me and didn't hear a word when they were talking to me. To others it looked as if I was in a coma."

Kristin took his hand and turned Nick towards her. "My darling Nick, you are such a beautiful man." There were tears in her eyes.

As they walked on, Nick continued to tell Kristin of the various things that he and Nicholas had said and done at various points along the way. He seemed to remember it all as if it was yesterday.

As they walked towards Newtimber Cottage, Nick told her how when he and Nicholas reached here they were both aching to go into the house, knowing that they could not.

They went inside and took a very loving shower together. Then, in bathrobes, they went downstairs and made a pot of tea. They took it into the garden and got the deckchairs. Normally, Kristin thought, they were very good at sitting together in comfortable silence. But this one wasn't comfortable.

"Nick, one of us has to put it into words. Do you think there is any possibility that you might die and flee away to your thirteen-year-old head tonight?"

"Have you been thinking about that as well? I'm so sorry, I should have told you straight away, but I just felt I couldn't. Yes, I've been thinking about this since yesterday morning. But I truly don't think it could happen because last time it happened in another universe, or so I believe. In our present universe none of the pre-conditions are the same. I have no need whatsoever to go back and try to prevent myself from having a horrible life. Because, in fact, thanks to many people, but especially to Nicholas, Alex and, my darling girl, to you, I have led a spectacularly beautiful and fulfilled life. I have a perfect daughter and two fantastic grandsons. I love you perhaps more than you will ever know, my darling Kristin, and I have no intention of leaving you yet; we have far too much exciting living to do still."

"I know darling; I know you have no intention."

§

That night when they went to bed they made love. It was very intense and beautiful. As they prepared for sleep Nick could hear the hoot of a tawny owl and, a little further away, the bark of a fox. He felt marinated in contentment.